Getting
Ghosted

Amelia Dax

For permissions contact: admin@ameliadax.com

Cover by Amelia Dax

ISBN: 978-1-990499-28-9

ACKNOWLEDGMENTS

I am surrounded by the best people who encourage me
on this crazy adventure.
I am thankful to you all. All day. Every day.

Amelia Dax

JUDGING JUDY

Of all the fuckin 'places I thought I'd end up, this is not one of them.

I have glasses, damn it. Made of brass or at least something that looks like brass. Anyway, no one who looks as smart as I do should end up in a place like this. As they pulled me from the box, I could see my sleek fur, golden and shiny under the fluorescent light in the beveled mirror. The rim of my glasses glinting a subtle nod to my superior intelligence.

I loved my elevated station in life.

At least, that's what I thought it was when they first hung me high on the wall to lord over my surroundings. Until they moved away and I finally saw it and realized the horrible joke the fates had played on me.

My final resting place… was attached to a wall overlooking a fucking toilet.

How is this dignified?

How did this even happen?

I was part of a set of noble creatures. We were articulate, intelligent, ready to inspire the world.

Some of my companions, who had been packed away with me, ended up on the wall in the children's section of the bookstore-cafe. Others positioned above the door to bid farewell to customers as they left. There was even one down by the fireplace watching over writing groups sipping coffee and offering advice, or parents playing Uno with their children.

Why did I end up here?

Amelia Dax

When I first entered this room, I had high hopes. The wallpaper depicted book spines lined up on a bookshelf as if the room itself had a high IQ. Even the mirror didn't immediately tip me off. I thought perhaps I'd found myself in a speaker's waiting room, where they'd do their final preparations before making a presentation.

Instead, I was reminded of that old schoolyard poem.

Sometimes I sits and thinks,
Sometimes I shit and stinks.

What did I do to deserve this? This had to be one of the rings of hell.

To make matters worse, after they mounted me on the wall, the door swung closed behind them and I was accosted with the sight of this absurd painting of a cat with its head tilted quizzically like an idiot. The caption on the bottom read: Are you pooping?

Seriously, what the actual fuck is that? Why, in the name of all that's holy, is that my chamber mate? Was it too much to ask for a volume of poems or a series of short stories as a companion in this dungeon? This was a bookstore, after all.

Resigned to my fate, I averted my eyes as much as I could every time someone came in to use the facilities. It wasn't very effective, considering my gaze was frozen in place.

It wasn't too bad when the men came in. Their backs were to me and most of them understood how to work a zipper and didn't drop their trousers in front of me. But I have to say I'm astounded at their lack of direction.

I'm a fox, without opposable thumbs and I dare to say, I would still have better aim.

The women were something entirely different. They sat facing me, giving me an often-unobstructed view of their valley of treasure.

If I was a lesser class of man... fox... err entity embalmed within this mask of brass, I would be in heaven. But an intellectual such as myself, with a high moral fiber, found it more than a little distressing.

Luckily, the foot traffic in my area was quiet that day. As I listened to the conversation flowing as people passed the door to my chamber. I understood they were preparing for the bookshop-café's grand opening.

Later that first night, after the lights blinked out, I heard snickers.

Someone was still here.

The last person leaving had apparently invited her ride home to come inside. I heard the lock click faintly behind them, and then more giggles.

"We shouldn't be doing this in here." A male voice said.

"Don't worry. No one can see inside. The paper is still up on the windows."

"But what if they come back?"

"Don't be such a worry wort. Everyone's gone. I'm the last one out." Her words seemed to satisfy his worry because the next thing I heard was the springs creak on one of the couches, intermixed with more giggles and the rustle of clothing.

This went on long enough for me to get irritated at being forced to be an unwilling audience when I heard the woman whisper-scream, "Oh, shit."

There was a frantic scramble and then rushing footsteps in my direction. Suddenly, two people were in my room, pressed tightly against the wall beneath me, with the door partially closed behind them for camouflage.

The lights flickered on in the main room. I'll only be a moment another female voice said as footsteps echoed through the empty bookstore-cafe toward the back, where these two miscreants hid.

The man nearly dislodged me from my hanger as they tucked their bare asses, which now glowed brightly in the hall's light, closer to the wall to avoid detection. The man's big foot nearly knocked over the garbage can, but luckily the new arrival was saying something else to their friend waiting by the outer door, so I don't think they heard.

The office door opened, and the lights turned on. The footsteps echoed away and then came back very quickly, plunging the office into darkness once again. The person didn't glance left, which was a good thing for the people hiding beside me.

They would have been caught for sure. Even though neither of them were very thick, there wasn't a whole lot of room to hide in the bathroom's small confines.

The footsteps walked back out to the front door. There was a click as the key put the deadbolt in place and then barely audible footsteps left.

The two people in my vicinity let out their collective breaths and burst out laughing. "Holy shit, that was close."

"That would have been so bad." The woman said as she flipped on the bathroom light, which made me finally understand the precariousness of the situation. She was holding her pants in her hand. Her shirt was unbuttoned, as was the front clasp of her bra.

He was still so hard he could have used his knob as a coat hanger for the jacket he was holding in front of him. I didn't see his trousers. They must have been still out in the couch area.

Yeah, there was no way to explain away their attempt to defile the bookstore-café if the other person had seen them.

"We should go." She started to put herself together again, but he put his hand on top of hers and guided it to his erection.

"We might as well finish what we started." he said. "I can't walk out of here like this."

The potential exhibitionism and getting caught seemed to have made him even harder. He sat down on the toilet and leaned back. "Come on, babe. We can finish this." He pulled on his thick cock and pre-come glistened as it slid from its tip.

She didn't take much convincing. She dropped her pants and shrugged off her still open blouse, then stepped over his lap to straddle him.

"Hang on," he stopped her. "Turn around so you don't hit your knees."

"Good idea."

She stepped back, turned around to give me a full frontal view no matter how hard I tried to avert my eyes. She was almost as tall as me. Slender hips and high perky breasts that seemed to defy gravity. She sat down on what would have been his lap, had his one-eyed monster not been in the way. She paused in a semi-squat while he positioned himself under her.

"Oh, yeah." He groaned as she slid down his pole.

This new position afforded me the chance to see everything. He was buried in her so deeply, it looked like they were her balls instead of his.

"Fuck, that feels good," she said as she balanced herself by putting her hand on the faux bookshelf wall as she rose on her toes to give him the space to move beneath her.

With her legs spread wide and her shirt gone, I could see her tits bounce with every thrust. He slid his hands up over her ribcage and massaged her breasts, and she leaned forward slightly to plant her feet more firmly on the floor so she could slide up and down on his rod.

"So good." She sighed as he tweaked her nipples. Pinching and pulling them slightly as she rode his cock. She reached down as she spread her knees even wider to give her better access to his balls.

He let out a low groan as soon as her fingers began fondling them. "Are you close?" he asked. "I can't hold out much longer." He dropped one of his hands below her waist and stroked his way down between her legs, pushing his finger in between her lips until she let out a squeak.

It was so satisfying when a man could find his woman's clit. Especially first try. I was proud of him as he expertly put just enough pressure on that precious little nub to make her hips start thrusting forward and back, instead of up and down, as she grew more aroused and began chasing her orgasm.

"Cum for me baby." he bit into her shoulder gently at the same time as he tweaked her nipple. With the extra stimulation and his finger still on her clit, she screamed as her orgasm hit.

He grunted behind her as she lost her rhythm, but he made-up for it by plowing into her from below. One, two, three quick strokes and his movements became jerky and erratic as he pumped his load into her.

When he stilled, she leaned back into his chest, and his arms came around her. Giving me the unobstructed view as his cum escaped from between their bodies, it was the sexiest sight.

One to make me wish I could extend my tongue out far enough to take a lick myself.

He held her close from behind and rained kisses down along her neck and across the shoulder that he'd bitten. They stayed that way until he softened enough to nearly pop out from her channel.

"Babe, I gotta move." she said, and he put his hands on her hips to help her up. Her legs wobbled a little as she moistened some paper towel to clean herself up before putting her clothes back on.

He grabbed some toilet paper and then had to spend time picking the pieces off of his still sticky cock.

"Why?" I questioned the heavens. "Why do guys always go for the toilet paper when there is water and a perfectly good paper towel right there?"

Once they were presentable again, except for his pants, of course, which were somewhere out in the main area, she straightened her hair before they stepped out of the bathroom.

Gallantly, he held his hand out for her to take to help her down the stairs, and I heard the two of them move away. More rustling as they found his trousers that had been shoved under the couch. Luckily, far enough out of sight that the person who interrupted them hadn't seen them.

More footsteps and another click of the lock, and I was finally alone. Except for that damn cat, who was now staring at me from the half-closed bathroom door.

The next day was grand opening day.

Amelia Dax

I was happy for them but dismayed for myself because this meant my chamber was about to be a lot busier since it would be more than just staff using it.

Halfway through the day, a couple of giggling teenagers. Honestly, they couldn't have been more than seventeen, came into the room together and locked the door behind them. Like the couple the night before, they didn't seem to mind the close confines.

The young woman hopped up on the vanity which creaked underneath her weight, not that she weighed that much, but it wasn't built for a person. She smiled as she hiked up her skirt and spread her legs.

If my mouth worked, I would have gasped as I saw her naked flesh underneath her mini skirt and thigh highs.

For Pete's sake. It was snowing outside. I heard the constant hum of complaint about the weather as people waited for their lattes and macchiato. That girl must have been freezing her bits off.

I was so concerned about her I failed to notice that the young fellow was busy undoing his pants and then, without any preparation, foreplay or consideration, he jammed himself into her.

"Ouch." If I had legs, I would have reflexively crossed them.

Instead of screaming at him or fighting him off for his roughness, she giggled and leaned back. Thumping her head against the mirror, nearly knocking it off the wall, she moaned. "Oh yeah, baby."

He smiled and pounded into her cunt. No finesse. No discernible technique. I think getting mauled by a rabid dog would have been more pleasurable.

8

Amelia Dax

Not that I actually wanted to see them go at it or judge their performance, but surely to God, the girl deserved more.

She didn't seem to agree. She gave out a high-pitched little squeak every time he entered her as she wrapped one leg up around his waist and braced her other foot against the doorknob so she wouldn't slide off the vanity between his thrusts.

I really regretted my eyes being cast in place because I desperately wanted to roll them. I mean, if I was going to be forced to be an observer, at least give me something good to watch.

Thankfully, it was over in about forty-five seconds. He gave a couple of grunts and then pulled away, leaving her to readjust quickly so she didn't fall off.

It didn't surprise me at all when the young fellow used toilet paper to clean himself up while leaving her to fend for herself.

"Oh honey. You deserve so much better." I wanted to tell her. She hopped off the vanity and swiveled onto the toilet and peed in front of him.

Then they were off giggling as they opened the door, eagerly talking about another grand opening they'd seen online. Apparently, it was a game they played. The challenge? To hit every grand opening, they could and christen the bathrooms.

Erm. It's good to have a goal, I guess.

If this was what my life was going to be like, I'd need to find a way to fall off the wall and break. Surely, this fake plastic brass I'd been created from would shatter and put me out of my misery.

9

The day was a steady stream of people coming into the bookstore-café. Some bought coffee. Many came in to visit me while they relieved themselves of said coffee and then went on their merry ways without any sexy-time.

Yay for me.

The staff jokingly started to refer to me as Judy.

This confused me because I was obviously male. Or I would be if I had a body to go with my face.

It was the third time someone called me Judy before I finally heard the explanation. There was a popular TV judge, named Judy, who didn't put up with any bullshit. I smiled. That description definitely fit me. I'd been judging people hard since I'd been hung on the wall.

A distressing number of customers were guilty of walking out after doing their business without washing their hands.

Not the staff, of course. They were diligent. I had to give props where props were due.

And it wasn't all bad. There were the cutest little kids coming in with their moms or their dads to do their business. One little guy got really distressed that he wasn't quite tall enough to stand on his own and hit the toilet bowl, so his dad lifted him up and then took an extra few minutes to clean up the dribbles on the floor. All while gently telling the youngster if he made a mess, he had to clean it up.

When he finished, the little one took the paper towel his dad had used out of the wastebasket and smeared the pee all over the floor again.

His dad cleaned that up, too. Good job.

Later, I wasn't sure what was going on in the main cafe, but it was some sort of opening night festivity. I could hear the booming voice, amplified by a microphone, welcoming everybody. In the midst of the chaos beyond my doors, I had another couple sneak into the bathroom.

Immediately, my interest was piqued.

The first guy was tall and slender, and he had a great ass. He almost had a cowboy vibe happening, with those tight jeans and a tucked in flannel shirt. All that was missing was the cowboy hat, but a true cowboy wouldn't wear his hat inside, anyway.

His companion was shorter and more barrel chested. Sadly, his ass was a lot flatter.

Hey, if they were going to call me Judy, I was going to judge.

To his credit, though, it was still cute. It was one of those butts that was almost perky at the top and then drifted off into nothing as it blended into his legs. I know this because he was also wearing tight jeans. Only his had a fair bit of spandex woven into the fabric. Skinny jeans, I think they called them. Skinny wasn't exactly the word I'd use for him. His muffin top was more like a cake top, but there I go judging again.

I wasn't going to judge because it was two men coming into my chamber, at least as long as they performed better than that young couple earlier in the afternoon. I'd resigned myself that if I was going to have to suffer through forced voyeurism, I was going to come up with the grading scale.

As soon as the door closed and locked behind them, they kissed with a little tongue, lots of passion, and even more smiles. Already these two were scoring higher than either of the previous two couples.

"Are you sure we should do this?" The taller one asked his partner.

11

The shorter man smiled confidently. "Honey, I've been watching you all night as you sashayed around in those jeans. I'm not going to make it until we get home."

The cowboy smiled. "I'm not sure I can make it, either. My jeans have been uncomfortable all night. You turn me on so much."

They kissed again as the shorter one reached down and undid the cowboy's buckle, then work his jeans down exposing that gorgeous ass of his.

God knows I loved a good ass, and I didn't care if it's male or female. His was a spectacular specimen.

"Bend over the vanity." His partner instructed as he raised the flannel shirt and the T-shirt underneath and then kissed the length of the cowboy's spine while he gripped and massaged those ass cheeks in his massive hands. Once his lips hit the base of the taller man's back, his thumbs spread those cheeks wide and continued kissing his way into the crack. He closed his eyes in bliss as he readied his partner.

Now see, that's the way you do it. I mentally scolded the teens from that afternoon. You get your partner good and ready before plunging yourself into their depths.

The cowboy immediately started squirming with pleasure as he raised upon his toes to give his friend better access. He braced his weight on one hand and started jerking himself off with the other. He was just tall enough that his balls cleared the edge of the sink, giving him room. I just hope he didn't damage his cock on the faucet. He wasn't a short guy in any way.

The quick view I got of him was that his tip extended an inch or two beyond his large palm. I'll admit, I salivated a little.

My gaze landed back on the fellow going for gold. His moans as he ate the ass of his partner threatened to drown out the microphone-amplified voice out in the main bookstore-café. His eyes were closed in ecstasy as he prepped his partner.

His hand was already wrapped around his shaft, pumping himself. He wasn't nearly as long as his companion, but his girth was impressive. His short, thick fingers barely reached the entire way around. No wonder he was prepping his partner well.

He gave one last lick and left a bubble of drool as he lifted his head. The slick stream snapped as he stood quickly and worked a finger, then two, into the puckered entrance. Lubing his digit with the per-cum he'd gathered from his own prick.

The cowboy sighed happily at the intrusion, bent his knees to match his partner's height and pushed his ass back, impaling himself on both digits exploring his ass. "Now." He whisper-screamed. "I need you inside me. Now."

Needing no further encouragement, the short man positioned his cock at his friend's entrance and pressed inside. He paused just after the initial breech for a moment, allowing the cowboy to adjust to his presence in his chute. Then he backed out and slid in further.

I watched his flat ass clench as he pulled back and then in again. At each thrust, I lost sight of his cock as he moved his hips forward. Which wasn't really a loss, because the tightening and releasing up his glutes was arousing to watch on its own. Hell, if I had a body, I'd be jerking myself off right now at the sight as his strokes got longer and began to pick up a rhythm.

The shorter guy placed his hands on his friend's hips one holding him in place while the other hand slid around to fondle his partner who immediately gave up control of his cock to place a second hand back on the vanity for support as his knees wobbled from the sensations and dropped against the small cupboard's doors.

Unlike the teenagers earlier, these two kept their gasps and moans quiet. The suppressed passion made it even more sexy to me.

The taller one in front threw his head back in ecstasy as I watched spurts of his cum land in the sink.

This set off his friend behind, who pulled out, as if purposefully letting me see his last few strokes of his rock-hard cock as he spurted over his friend's ass and the shirttails of his flannel shirt still flipped up over his back.

As the last soft grunt echoed through the tiny room, the tall cowboy turned around, leaving a slick trail of come across his partner's stomach. The two men embraced. Their leisurely kiss was still filled with passion as they eased themselves back into reality.

Not two seconds later, someone knocked on the door.

Their eyes flashed with mirth as they quickly cleaned each other up and tucked themselves back into their jeans. One more quick peck on the lips before they exited the bathroom down the stairs.

The white-haired woman who came in after them had heard what they'd been doing. As she entered the room, she had a smirk on her face. "Those dirty, dirty little boys." She looked around the room. Too bad I can't set up a camera. Her laugh was genuine, "I could get some great ideas for an erotica."

I smiled at her comment. Oh, the stories I could already tell her.

Soon the night finished, tables were cleared, floors were washed and my chamber was scrubbed from top to bottom. Eventually the light was turned out and the bookstore-café was silent.

Not bad for my first day. I thought to myself. This wasn't going to be nearly as bad as I thought it would be.

Amelia Dax

Amelia Dax

HAUNTED APARTMENT

Being dead sucked.

It really did. I didn't have control over anything. I was stuck in this apartment. No matter how much I tried to leave it. I couldn't even go out into the hall. My only escape had been to lean out the window to catch a glimpse of a life that was passing me by.

Alas, even that small respite ended back when some safety guy in the seventies decided that it was too dangerous to have windows open any higher than the sixth floor. They sealed them all shut except for the ones which doubled as fire escapes.

Unfortunately for me, I didn't crash through that particular window during the construction accident that killed me. So, it might as well be a brick wall as far as I was concerned.

I've wanted to escape ever since I died in this apartment. I've been here for almost eighty years. The last couple of years living… err, existing, with the current tenant has been absolute hell for me.

It wasn't so bad at first when the guy moved in, but then he started dating a woman who was the spitting image of my wife the last time I saw her. She was so young and pretty, with blond hair and big blue eyes.

I can't describe how horrible it felt to see someone who resembled my wife look at him with the same loving gaze my wife used to have when looking at me.

To make it worse, for all I knew, this woman could be my great-granddaughter. My wife and I had a little boy, and she was pregnant when I died. It killed me to know I had a whole family out there somewhere who I knew nothing about.

Knowing there was a possibility she was kin added an extra eww-factor. Especially when they made out on the couch and then started having sex. Part of me wanted to scream at him to stop kissing my wife's look-a-like, while the rest of me wanted to protect the virtue of the girl who could be my great grandchild.

Did I mention I couldn't leave?

The best I could do was to turn my back and walk down the short hallway of the tiny apartment. My only salvation was that the walls had been built and properly insulated before contractors started to cheap out on building supplies.

When the couple finally made it to the bedroom, the sounds were at least muffled.

Then they got married, and she moved in.

It was a special type of torture. Especially once she got pregnant. It was like I had a front-row seat to watch somebody else living the life I should have had. It was really hard not to be resentful. I didn't know what I'd done in a past life to deserve such cruel treatment from fate.

Then came the day I'd been waiting for and strangely dreading as her due date approached. They started looking at houses. I had mixed feelings when I watched them pack up to leave, knowing I'd never get to see the baby. A little girl, who was possibly my great-great-granddaughter.

It took a while for the landlord to rent the apartment again. They took a couple of months to do some renovations. Oddly enough, they installed new windows with angled openings and screens. I still couldn't see down to the street, but at least I could feel fresh air on my face again. Once the construction crews went home for the night, I'd wander around, inspecting their work and marvel at the new-fangled way they installed things. Some methods were really neat. Others left me shaking my head, wondering what the hell they were thinking.

They did a good job, though. The building was old and needed constant maintenance. I'd been on the construction crew that built it back in the day. That's how I died. I fell off the 8th floor while we were shifting the forms to pour the cement for the next story, when I tripped over a toolbox and went flying over the edge. Thanks to my safety rope I only fell two stories.

Unfortunately, the angle of my fall made me crash into the gaping hole where they were about to install windows. My head hit the window frame.

I never got to see my wife again or hold our new baby. I sat in shock as the workers moved around where my body had lain and watched them finish building. Over the decades, I'd shared this space with at least a dozen couples and half as many single tenants.

My desolation grew with each new renovation and roommate who was completely unaware of my existence... until she walked in.

Perhaps fate decided to reward me for my patience.

This time, the potential tenant who came in to see the place with the landlord looked nothing like my wife. This broad, Gracie, he called her, was easily five-foot-ten, with a rack that defied gravity. The swell of her hips made my cock swell for the first time in over thirty years.

To my delight, she got the apartment instead of the butt-ugly bachelor with bad teeth who still played with toy soldiers on a Saturday night. I know this because that's what he told the landlord as he was being shown around.

I can't fault the landlord for choosing the woman, either.

The next weekend, the tall brunette moved her belongings into my space with the help of three large frat boys. To my surprise, they seemed to pay as much attention to each other as to her. I watched their interaction with keen interest because it boggled my mind that she wasn't the center of their focus. I mean, this woman had it going on from head to toe.

As they finished setting up the bed, I guess they weren't as immune as I thought they were. The fellow closest to her, Ian, I think his name was, picked her up and threw her onto the mattress, following her down. He slid one hand under her shirt as he buried his face between her neck and shoulder.

She laughed as she pounded his back. "Get off me, you brute." He backed away a little, but I think it was more because Andrew, one of the other guys, joined them on the bed. Ian shifted far enough to give them room to undo her pants.

The third man, Brad, just stood there for a beat, then stripped off his shirt and then tore his sweatpants down his legs, taking his underwear with them. Stark naked, he stood there watching, waiting for his turn while slowly pumping his massive cock with his hand.

The first guy, Ian, was already taking her sweatshirt off.

Andrew peeled her jeans down her legs, then didn't waste any time ripping off her lacy little panties and diving headfirst between her legs. Before he blocked my view, I saw that she was bare as the day she was born. There didn't seem to be any stubble at all. I know because I was leaning into the room as far as I could.

Honestly, I was a little shocked that I was able to do more than tilt my head in. The bedroom had always been beyond my reach before.

She arched back to give Ian room to take off her bra. It was tossed to the side as his big hands hid her magnificent tits from view. He leaned in to kiss her deeply as her arms wrapped around his shoulders.

Brad still stood there pulling on his pud, patiently waiting his turn.

Gracie spread her legs wide and started gyrating her hips as Andrew continued to eat her out like a pro until she arched her back again and let out an intense scream that was muffled by Ian's kiss.

Still, it was loud enough that I'm sure the neighbours, whose bedroom was on the other side of the wall, heard.

Ian switched his attention to her breasts and started sucking the tips of each of them, while Andrew moved away so that Brad could line himself up with her entrance, now that she was nice and wet.

She was still breathing hard as Brad kneeled between her legs, licked his thumb to circle her clit before lining himself up and plunging into her with one slow, smooth motion. He was so thick I half expected to be able to trace his progress up over her taut belly.

She sighed in contentment when he reached the hilt and paused to let her stretch around his girth. Then, when she was ready, she wound her legs around his hips, crossing her legs behind his ass as if to make sure he wasn't able to escape.

Not that he looked like he had any intention of leaving his spot between her legs.

I'd lost track of Andrew for a moment until he walked up the side of the bed and kneeled beside Gracie's head. He was naked now, too. He reached under her shoulder as she pulled herself up, using his arm for leverage until she could swallow the broad end of his cock. She balanced on her elbow and used her other hand to grip the base of his dick to reach where her lips couldn't quite make it.

The man was huge.

I mean, I was no slouch in that department, but that guy was truly impressive.

With her movement, Ian had been nudged out of the picture, but that didn't faze him at all. He just stripped down and waited for his turn.

Andrew motioned him up toward the head of the bed and in what seemed to have been a well-practiced move, he stood on the bed, braced his hands on the ceiling, which brought his short pudgy cock level with Andrew's mouth. Andrew swallowed him whole.

I saw Ian's knees shake and thought it was a good thing he had the foresight to brace himself against the ceiling, otherwise it would have been disastrous for all of them.

Despite my comparatively tame life, I was no stranger to this type of action. Back in the sixties, everyone was fucking. Girls. Guys. It didn't matter. If you had an orifice, it was plugged with somebody's cock or sucked by somebody's mouth.

Let's just say I've definitely received an education since my death in nineteen-forty-nine.

Gracie leaned back against Ian's leg and raised her hand to fondle his balls while she continued to suck on Andrew's cock.

Andrew's hand was splayed over Ian's ass to help hold them both steady while Brad continued to pound away between Gracie's legs.

The push and pull between them all was like an intricate ballet.

My gaze darted back and forth in case I missed something. Moans of pleasure were muffled by mouths full of each other.

Somehow, Brad slid his way up Gracie's body to suckle at her tits without getting in the way. I was certain he'd get a hair full of jizz if Gracie wasn't able to swallow fast enough when Andrew came.

It wouldn't take long. Strokes were shorter, and movements grew more erratic with every bump and grind.

The guys seemed determined to make sure Gracie was the first to get off. Even though this would be her second orgasm of the night.

Andrew slowed down his mouth action on Ian and Brad rose on his knees again, his hands tweaking the peak of Gracie's tit with one hand and thumbed her clit with what I guessed from her ecstatic noises around Andrew's cock was the exact amount of pressure she needed as he plowed into her with quick powerful strokes.

Her legs suddenly straightened as a scream escaped around the huge-assed cock in her mouth.

Andrew eased his hips away from her until it plopped down against his leg, then back up again, to give her a chance to catch her breath as her orgasm faded.

Brad leaned forward again, bracing himself on his forearms and took Andrew into his mouth as his body covered Gracie, keeping her warm and cuddled as she came back to earth.

Without realizing it, I'd moved farther into the room until I laid down on the bed with Gracie. With a near audible click that sent a wave of shock through me, my body settled in the same space she occupied, with none of them being the wiser. Incredulously, I shared her view of the men still frolicking above her.

Andrew sucked Ian as Brad's throat moved up and down as he swallowed Andrew's cock until he came.

Even though I wasn't gay, I appreciated the poetry of the motion around me. Especially when Andrew let out a howl around Ian's cock. Followed by Ian's spunk raining down on Gracie's head as Andrew's lips lost their grip around Ian's thick head.

Amateur. I laughed to myself. As if I had any experience with holding a man's cock in my mouth.

My body felt heavy. Which was odd. I tried to sit up but discovered I couldn't. I was trapped in the same space as Gracie.

I panicked. Arms and legs flailed as I tried to release myself from the weight that enveloped me.

Unaware of my plight. Ian stepped off the bed and Brad eased his body toward its foot to give Gracie, and apparently me, room to sit up.

I could feel Ian's cum slide down over Gracie's chin and drip onto her upper chest. It was the oddest sensation.

Why the fuck was I feeling it?

I tried to get up from the bed again, but I was stuck. I couldn't move my arms or legs. I seemed to be tied to Gracie and couldn't move unless she moved.

Brad bent down to kiss Gracie.

Kiss us? Why did I feel his lips against my skin, as if it were my own?

Then his tongue darted out to lick her face clean and then gave her open-mouthed kisses to her chest, vacuuming up the salty drops from Ian's cock.

I felt every nip and suck.

Gracie wove her hands through Brad's short hair, and I felt his stiff strands against the palm of my hand. Our hands?

What the hell was happening?!

I wasn't complaining, not really. I loved finally being able to touch another person and be touched by them. I would have preferred to have been absorbed into one of the guys and feel Gracie's body. But I wasn't upset at being part of Gracie.

The teenaged boy inside my head was thrilled at the idea of being able to play with her tits whenever I wanted to. Assuming I could convince her to pleasure herself.

Before I could check to see if I had any control over her actions, the three naked men surrounded her. They pulled her up to her feet and the four, well, five of us, did a shuffle step towards her shower.

Part of me wanted to revolt against the feeling of these naked men with their huge cocks brushing my skin within Gracie's body.

Brad was behind us with his hands on Gracie's hips as he steered the group toward the bathroom. His still chubby prick pressed into the small of our back.

Ian stepped ahead of us to open the door, and then he reached into the tub to turn on the shower.

I had no idea how this was going to work. This was not a big shower. The four of us would have to stand closer than we already were. There was hardly enough room for one person.

Andrew stepped in first once the water was hot, and he guided Gracie in so that our back was braced up against his front. He was a little shorter than the other two guys, so his cock teased at the crack of her ass.

I couldn't decide if it felt better or worse for me. I wasn't a prude, but I wasn't sure if I was ready to experience anything through the back door.

The other two each kept one foot on the bathroom floor and put the other into the tub. Angling their bodies to block any spray that escaped past the shower curtain in an attempt to keep the water from pooling on the floor.

And then everyone was moving at once. Somehow Andrew got shampoo. I think Ian helped him from the other side of the shower stall from Brad. He poured a long dollop from the bottle and began massaging the soap into Gracie's scalp while the other two men shared the bottle of body wash and started gliding their hands over Gracie's body, making sure her every hill and valley was completely clean.

I felt Gracie's arousal with every stroke from their hands.

Her skin was so soft, not like my hair-roughened chest. The sensations of their palms against her skin were unlike anything I'd ever felt before. The smooth slickness made every nerve ending come alive.

I love the silky feel of the soap as each of the men seemed to work over a different part of my body. Brad concentrated on my breasts while Ian reached down between our legs as Gracie moved her feet farther apart to give him better access.

Honestly. I'd never thought about what sex and arousal would feel like as a woman and I'm ashamed to say I never did this kind of thing for my wife.

Sure, times were different back then, but the way these men worshiped every part of Gracie's body made me sad I didn't try harder. They gave me a whole new appreciation for what could have been.

Andrew reached up to detach the handheld showerhead and then rinsed the shampoo from her hair.

Then Brad, or was it, Ian? I couldn't tell because Gracie had closed our eyes. One of them took the shower wand to rinse the soap from the rest of her body.

The water felt exquisite against our skin, especially as someone lifted her breasts and they used the soft spray underneath and then slowly drifted it over our stomach and then switched the stream to a higher pressure before continuing the journey between her legs.

Even though I still could feel my cock, I also felt every sensation she felt. Every touch was amplified until my body wanted to explode.

She leaned our body back against Andrew, who wrapped his arms around us. He must have been a fortune teller because an instant later, she bent her knees to allow the other two men even more access.

They alternated between running their fingers through her folds and teasing her opening with fingers nudging inside before changing tactics and spreading her lower lips open wide. They switched the water stream again, this time to a steady pulse and whoever was holding the wand expertly directed it to feel like it surrounded her clit.

The unexpected contact jolted us backward, further into Andrew's arms, as he tightened his hold to keep us from falling.

It sent fireworks from my dick to my toes. Every nerve ending felt like it was exploding in euphoria. As if my entire body was one huge, erogenous zone.

I gripped my cock, which was rock hard. I stroked myself. The stream from the shower head kept up its rhythm, expanding the sensation until I felt my balls empty against the shower curtain in front of Gracie.

It was as if her cunt and my cock had become one.

The sounds coming out of her throat and the sensations I felt coming from her let me know she came at the same time.

After the most powerful orgasm I'd ever experienced, the men continued on with their care.

The other two stepped fully into the shower and let her lean against them as Andrew put conditioner in her hair and then rinsed it out. Then, one by one, they stepped out of the shower, handing Gracie from one to the other until she was safely standing on the shower mat. Then they began toweling her down.

The soft fabric against my skin as they worked felt amazing.

Andrew continued with Gracie's hair while Brad and Ian made sure that her limbs and nether regions were completely dry.

I'd never felt so pampered. I thought they were done when I felt their hands, wet and slippery, against Gracie's skin. I wanted to open my eyes to see what they were doing, but Gracie was content to keep her eyes closed.

It wasn't until I smelled the slightly floral fragrance that I realized they were moisturizing her skin. Now I understood why women used moisturizer. It wasn't just to make their skin feel soft. The act of applying it was sensual, even more-so when she had three attentive men massaging it into her skin.

I had another chubby. The silkiness of the lotion combined with the roughness of their hands made me come on the spot embarrassingly fast. Gracie finally opened her eyes, and I was surprised Ian wasn't wearing my spunk from his belly button down to his thigh.

I guess that was the benefit of being a ghost. No one had to clean up my mess.

I leaned back as if to check in with Gracie to see if she felt my orgasm the same way I felt hers. In that respect, we still seemed to be separate. While she was definitely aroused again, she was not as relaxed as she would have been had she also orgasmed. Despite the heaviness and tension, I could feel building between her legs, her lithe limbs were languid as the men attended to her.

They sat her on a chair I'd seen them put in the bathroom earlier in the day. Its purpose baffled me at the time. Now I understood.

Ian on one side, Brad on the other, guided her to sit down.

Andrew picked up a wide-tooth comb from the vanity to comb out her hair.

I could feel the sensations as he worked the tangles free, but the way our bodies reacted was still separate. I felt tension through my spine and my thighs. The telltale pressure was already building in my balls.

Gracie was pleasantly aroused, but mostly relaxed.

The other two men kneeled at her feet and started applying moisturizer to her ankles and instep.

The sensation tickled so much I wanted to raise my knees and kick them out of the way. It had been so many decades since someone had actually touched me, it's no wonder I was ultra-sensitive.

Gracie, on the other hand, just moaned in appreciation as she leaned back against the chair and let the boys straighten out her legs one at a time. They balanced them on their raised knees as they worked. Massaging the arch of her foot, calves and behind her knee before continuing up her inner thighs.

That's when I felt the tingling and pressure start to build between her legs. Her moans grew more urgent and frequent.

Meanwhile, I was about ready to blow my load again.

Gracie bent her knees slightly and shifted her legs as far apart as she could while the men massaged the lotion into her inner thighs and the surprisingly sensitive skin in the crease where her legs met her hips.

Once Andrew finished with her hair, he gathered it up in a clip and then began to rub lotion into her shoulders, as the other men worked their way closer to her cunt. He gradually slid his hands down her front to massage her breasts. He leaned down over her shoulder and raised her tits to his mouth.

It was the oddest sensation for me to have his hands lift my chest and then his warm mouth engulf my nipples.

Gracie's nipples.

He moved back and forth between them.

The difference between the humid heat suction and then the sudden cool air when he switched sides left the tips almost sore to the touch, yet standing tall, begging for more.

On the breast not in his mouth, his thumbs circled our nipples, without touching them.

I wanted to scream. "Enough with the teasing already."

Still, he persisted. Around and around, he twirled his thumbs. Deliberately ignoring the sensitive nubs at the peak.

Then Brad and Ian shifted positions again as Gracie and I watched through her hooded eyelids.

Andrew let go of our breasts for a moment and I felt the back of the chair recline a few inches.

Gracie smiled as if she knew what was coming next.

It was Ian's turn to settle between our legs while Brad continued to massage her outer lips and separated them to give Ian access to delve into the treasure trove between her legs.

Ian wasted no time. He nudged his shoulders between her thighs and licked at her exposed pussy. He tunneled his tongue to enter her channel before taking the slickness from there and deposited it around her clit as his tongue circled the bundle of nerves.

My entire body clenched as the sensations bombarded me from what felt like every angle.

He lifted his head far enough to give him room to take his big index finger and tease around her entrance. His thumb circled over her clit to make sure she was slick before he pushed his digit further into her channel. He stroked her a few times, never taking his eyes from her face as he watched her reactions. Making sure she was enjoying his attentions and adjusting his actions to repeat a motion if it made her gasp in pleasure.

I was going out of my mind. I wasn't sure how much more I could take before my entire being dissolved into the ether as Ian slowly slid in and out of her tight hole. I felt every inch of him as he crooked his finger and hit a spot that made Gracie's entire body jump.

He concentrated on that spot until Gracie, and I were both quivering with pleasure.

I felt Brad stand before he bent over Andrew's hands, that were still massaging Gracie's breasts. Then his lips met mine.

I'd never kissed a man before, even though it was Gracie's lips he thought he was kissing. I felt him nip at my bottom lip and then dive into her open mouth as she let out a sigh.

There was so much love and passion between the four of them I felt like an interloper, yet welcomed as one of them, even though none of them knew I was there.

Ian replaced his fingers with his cock. He stretched Gracie... and me, as he entered our shared entrance inch by excruciating inch.

The heavy full feeling was as natural as it was foreign to me as my balls tightened yet again. I wondered how many times I could come before I'd fade away into nothing.

It didn't take long before his strokes became shorter and quicker.

Andrew's hands didn't stop moving over her stomach and hips while Brad had taken control of her breasts and continued to kiss us as if there was no tomorrow.

They shifted one last time. Andrew had one hand on his own cock and Brad shifted to the side to give Andrew room to step forward.

Gracie turned her head, and we both engulfed Andrew's length in her mouth.

I almost gagged when he thrust deeply across my tongue and hit the back of my throat.

Gracie was obviously more used to having a cock in her mouth, swallowed around him and used her tongue underneath his glans, a move I recognized my wife had done on the rare time I could get her to experiment.

Now, I appreciated it from the other side.

The men were moaning.

Gracie opened her eyes a little and I could see Andrew and Ian embracing each other and exchanging a soulful kiss.

Another stroke from Ian and Gracie set off the second chain reaction of the day.

Ian pulsed inside Gracie, which had us squeezing her muscles as our own orgasm erupted in waves of pleasure. I vaguely registered Brad's release hitting Gracie's stomach as Andrew's cock spewed in our mouth.

Gracie tilted her head back a fraction as she worked her throat to swallow his entire load. She didn't open her mouth to let him go for several moments. Not until I could feel him softening.

When everyone caught their breath, the three men helped Gracie up to her feet.

Brad grabbed a fresh face cloth and ran it under warm water to clean her up and then they led her back to her freshly made bed.

I don't even know which one of the guys escaped long enough to make it. I was so caught up in what was happening.

They tucked her in. Each giving her a lingering kiss goodnight before putting their clothes back on and letting themselves out of her apartment.

I curled up contentedly along with Gracie and listened to her breath even out as she fell asleep. As exhausted as I was from this new experience, my mind was racing. If this was the way I was going to spend the rest of my days, I couldn't wait.

Amelia Dax

Amelia Dax

FROM THE SHADOWS

I often sat on my deck, looking out over the bay of Fundy. It was quiet, peaceful, and very lonely. Life hadn't gone as expected. My plan had never been to live in this house, with only my dog for company.

I let my thoughts wander as I gazed into the trees.

The breeze constantly changed the pattern of shadows as the leaves and evergreens shifted against each other. It made for a fun game of shape-seeking, like we did as kids, laying on a field, searching the sky for silhouettes of dogs or dragons among the clouds drifting by.

To break the silence, I'd often talk to myself or have one-sided conversations with my old pup, Dash. A misnomer. He didn't dash anywhere these days.

One night as I watched the shadows play in the trees, a patch of dark seemed to change shape. "Is that a dog or a deer?" I asked my drowsy companion, and to my surprise, a deer stepped out of the shadows and onto my lawn. I held my breath and soothed the napping dog on my lap to ensure he stayed quiet and didn't frighten the delicate animal as it picked its way across the grass and eventually disappeared into the shadows again.

It became a ritual. Something to help me pass the solitary evenings. I had friends, but I just couldn't be bothered to accept their invitations and go out. Each night, I'd shift my chair slightly to see a new grouping of branches and their shadows.

By the middle of October, the air grew cold after sunset. Not willing to give up the evenings on my deck, I bought a propane firepit.

Its glow cast a different type of light on the trees, which were now nearly barren of leaves.

That was when I first saw him.

The shadows of the evergreens and birch trees formed a silhouette of a man wearing a fedora, and if a twig moved just right, it looked like he was smoking a cigarette.

I always did love a good bad-boy.

Once I saw his shape in the foliage, I noticed it every time I looked in that direction. I stopped moving my chair around to keep him visible. Night after night, I'd see my man made of shadows and feel less lonely. Eventually, I started talking to him like I talked to my dog.

Who, I'm sure, didn't mind the shift in my attention so he could get in quality naptime at my feet.

I told the shadow about my days and explained the circumstances that brought me to live alone in this big old creaky house. I told him about my hopes and dreams, occasionally nodding off in the quiet of the evening.

Often, I would read by the firelight on my phone and the story would get so good my hand would slip beneath my pants and play with myself while I read the titillating words on the page about how the man's thick dick would plunge into her. I'd get wet reading about how he'd use a thumb to circle her clit to make sure she came before he did. My husband, may he rest in peace, used to do that for me.

Soon I got into the habit of reading my books aloud and one late September night that was unseasonably warm, took off my pants and spread my legs wide. I used my tiny bullet vibrator that I'd had the foresight to stick in my pocket. The combination of the soft buzz from my toy and what I could have sworn was the shadow shifting toward me as if paying attention gave me the best orgasm I've had in ages.

So, of course, you know I did it again the next night and the night after that.

October turned to November and then the time changed from Daylight Savings Time. It was dark by supper and too cold to sit outside, even with a jacket and a heavy blanket. It was especially too cold to play, despite the heat I generated between my legs.

Even though it was afternoon, I bade my imaginary companion goodbye for the winter and told him I hoped to see him again in the spring as I stored my patio furniture and small firepit in my garage.

The next night, we had the first Nor'Easter of the season. I let my old dog out on the deck, hoping he wouldn't make me go outside to carry him down to the lawn to do his business. He'd become really lazy lately.

Instead of waiting or waddling down the stairs, he bounded down the steps and ran around the house, disappearing into the darkness toward the road.

Cursing under my breath, I closed the patio door and rushed to grab his leash before going outside to chase after him. I didn't live on a busy road, but there were a few teens who felt the speed limit was barely a suggestion.

My hand was on the doorknob when a knock on the other side startled me enough to drop the leash I was holding.

Peeking out the side window, my porch light revealed a vaguely familiar, dark-haired man. His hat was dripping wet from the rain. He held my normally grumpy old dog carefully in his arms, and the animal licked his chin as if he was an old friend.

It shocked me. My dog hated everyone.

I opened the door to usher them both in from the storm.

"Dash was making a run for it." The man said as he put my dog down on the floor.

The animal shook out his fur, whined and wove himself around the man's legs before plopping down over his feet.

Laughing at my pet's antics, I debated the wisdom of inviting this kind stranger inside my home.

I knew I'd seen him before, but didn't know from where. He knew Dash's name, which made him local. Dash and I stopped going for long walks a long time ago.

The poor man wasn't wearing a jacket and was soaked to the skin after rescuing my dog.

Considering my pet's immediate trust of the man, I offered him a towel and invited him in for a cup of tea to warm up and to thank him for returning Dash to safety.

He thanked me as he closed the door behind him.

"Do you want me to toss your sweater in the dryer?" I asked as I filled the electric kettle.

"Yes, please. I doubt it will dry completely, but at least it will be warm when I put it back on." His T-shirt came off with his sweater.

I had intended to turn my back to give him some privacy, I was stopped short by the sight of his muscular torso.

He wasn't big and bulky. He had lean muscles and well-defined shoulders. When he realized he'd caught my attention, he straightened and may have sucked in his gut a little bit. He didn't have a dad-bod, yet he wasn't quite a six-pack either. His abs were defined and his pecks were amazing, hiding under the perfect amount of chest hair.

I have a thing about pecs. It annoys me to see a man work out his abs and shoulders and not define his chest.

This guy could have been carved from my dreams, especially with his slightly furry chest, just enough to keep me warm on a cold winter's night.

"Sorry I'll get the hot started, err start the boiling to water, I mean the water boiling." I stuttered and turned away. I could hear him chuckling behind me as the sound of the towel gliding over skin made my legs want to rub together. "Down girl." I chastised myself under my breath.

My dog didn't follow me, instead he stayed, wrapping himself around the stranger's feet. "I'm sure we've met before." I said trying to place him.

"I've been around for a while now," he said. "I don't get out and about much, but I saw your dog racing towards the street. I decided I'd better catch him before he got himself hurt."

"Thank you." I said to him. "I'd be lost without that mutt."

He chuckled and bent down to scratch my old dog between his ears. Dash leaned in against his legs, lifting his chin and sighed like he was in heaven.

I rolled my eyes and checked the kettle. "Traitor." I said and then raised my gaze to my handsome stranger.

Now that I'd actually looked higher than his chest, I realized just how handsome he was. Dark hair, slightly too long over the ears and nape of his neck. His eyes were as grey as the storm clouds in the sky. He'd draped my towel around his neck and was still holding his wet sweater and T-shirt in a ball.

"Give me those and I'll toss them in the dryer."

"Thank you." He said again as I nudged by him to the mudroom off to the side of the entryway.

I quickly looked for the tag to see what dryer setting was safe. When I didn't see one, I noticed the sweater looked handmade and felt like it was probably wool. I set the temperature to air dry. I'm not going to lie I was a little grateful to have the extra time to get to know him while his clothing dried. The suddenly horny part of me wanted to ask if he'd like me to dry his jeans, too.

Honestly, I was a little surprised at how aroused I was. Sure, it had been a couple of days since I used my toy out on the deck, but I shouldn't be this needy. Just this guy's proximity set my libido into overdrive. I decided I'd better rein myself in because I'd never been the type to have sex with a random stranger. I always preferred to have a relationship, even if it was just a friends-with-benefits scenario.

The kettle was boiling by the time I got back into the kitchen. He'd moved into the room and sat at my kitchen island, holding my dog in his arms. Comfortable in my space, as if he'd always been there.

Dash, my silly ancient pup, was busy lapping at his chin as if he was a long-lost friend who came to play. That settled my trepidation because there was a large part of me that thought I was nuts for inviting him into my house, a perfect stranger on a conveniently stormy night. Still, there was just something so familiar about him that made it hard to be distrustful.

"Do you want me to find you something to wear so you don't catch a chill?" The mature, responsible part of my brain thought to ask.

"It's really warm in here. I'm fine without."

Yes. Yes, you are. I pinched myself to get my errant thoughts back under control.

One cup of tea led to another. He was so easy to talk to. I felt like I'd known him for years. He knew of many people in the community, which further put me at ease.

The weather raged outside, and our pot of tea extended into munchies and a movie. Every time he leaned forward to grab his cup or a handful of popcorn, I was conscious of his warm skin sliding against my arm. The dryer had stopped over an hour ago, but neither of us suggested he put his shirt and sweater back on.

When the popcorn was finished he asked, "Do you mind if I…?" as he shifted toward me. His arm lifting over my head to rest along the back of the couch, behind my shoulders.

I dropped my head back to use his bicep as a pillow. "Mmm, comfy." I laughed.

He flexed his muscles, making me giggle like a schoolgirl as he pulled me closer to his naked chest.

"Ho-ly Hell." I'd be in so much trouble if he kept this up.

His skin was warm, and he sat close enough to make my tits perk up.

My nipples hardened into tight peaks. I wanted to rub against him. This was not me. Not how I usually acted.

I glanced down at my dog, only to realize there'd be no help from him to calm my libido.

Usually, if I invited a man over to my house and we started getting cozy, Dash was right there in the middle to ruin the mood.

Tonight, my pup lay sprawled on his dog bed in the corner, oblivious to my quandary of whether to be a responsible adult and offer the stranger his shirt back or if I should do what I really wanted and climb onto his lap and kiss him until we were breathless.

As if he could read my mind, he patted his lap. "I'm willing if you are, Darlin'."

41

Amelia Dax

I needed no second invitation. With his arm for support, and near miracle coordination, I rose, turned and swung my leg over his lap in one motion so I was face to face with him.

He reached under my ass and tugged me in closer to his body. His erect cock pressed solidly against the crevice between my legs as one of his big hands splayed across my back and the other slid up to my neck before he pulled me in for a kiss.

His lips were strong and firm under mine. There was nothing tentative about his technique as our mouths merged.

I gasped, and he took advantage. Our tongues danced against each other, perfectly matched. One of my hands grip the back of the couch. The other slid through the hair at the nape of his neck, weaving my fingers through the soft strands.

His hand slid up my rib cage and paused just under my breasts as if waiting for permission.

I bump my nose against his when I pulled back just far enough to say, "God yes, then kissed him again."

His hands cupped me before he held me steady with one hand and unzipped my hoodie with the other. In seconds, he pushed my plain cotton sports bra up and the warmth of his palms against my skin sent a jolt through me. I pressed down on his erection and rubbed against him.

Without breaking our kiss, he moved one of his hands toward the base of my spine and he flexed his hips to rise up and press against me

The pressure was amazing. I rode back and forth on his rigid length while he moved in rhythm to give me exactly the touch I needed.

42

"That's it darlin'." he whispered against my lips before capturing them again. "Take what you need from me." He trailed his nose down my jawline, over my collarbone, and between my breasts. Kissing his way over to one peak and then pressing my mounds together so he could easily go back and forth between my nipples. The hot, wet heat from his mouth and the cool air when he moved away was exquisite. I felt like a teenager under the bleachers at the gym dry humping while he stole second base, but I don't remember those fumblings ever feeling so good.

He moved again and my breath caught in my throat.

I bore down and swiveled my hips as the orgasm exploded between my legs.

He didn't move. He let me control the motion and take exactly what I needed. Not easing off the pressure until I was done.

I sagged against him and instead of pushing me away or demanding it was my turn to look after him, he just wrapped his arms around me and held me close. Skin to skin. I finally got to feel his magnificent chest against mine. He felt better than I'd hoped. Like. a big teddy bear.

Embarrassed by my wantonness, I started to move away.

He pulled me back toward him and held me close. "Not yet. Just give me one more minute."

My embarrassment fled at the need in his tone, and I relaxed against him again.

I must have fallen asleep, because the next thing I knew, the storm had eased and a quick glance at my watch showed it was three o'clock in the morning.

He was gone.

He'd put one of my decorative pillows under my head and covered me with the blanket that had been draped over the back of my couch.

It was such a sweet gesture, but then I worried my loneliness had made me too trusting. Panicked, I searched my house to make sure he hadn't robbed me. It filled me with relief to see my laptop and camera were still in their places on my desk.

Paranoid, I checked the locks on my doors and windows to ensure he hadn't been sneaky and left a way to break into my house later. Everything was secure.

He'd locked my doorknob on his way out. The only thing left to do was to turn the deadbolt and head upstairs to bed.

I fell asleep with a smile on my face and the hope I'd see him again.

The next evening, there was a knock at my door not long after the sun went down. He looked sheepish when I answered, proffering me a bouquet of late blooming wildflowers, only slightly beaten up by the storm the night before. "I hope you don't mind me stopping by again. I find myself at a crossroads, and I really enjoyed your company last night."

This time, he refused my offer of tea. We sat on the couch and chatted, our bodies leaning closer and closer until he pulled me over onto his lap, straddling his hips.

"Is this okay?" he asked, but I was already kissing his lips before he got the last part of his question out.

His arms wrapped around me, holding me steady as his lips left mine to trail down my neck

I arched my back against his strong hands offering access to the tops of my breasts peeking out over my low V-neck top which I might have worn in the hopes he'd return. If he hadn't, I'd planned to take Dash for a walk to see if I could find my mysterious stranger. I was grateful he saved me the trouble.

He nestled his face between my breasts and breathed deeply, inhaling my scent as if committing it to memory. "You are the most perfect woman I've ever seen," he whispered. "I can't believe I get to hold you."

A little later, in a bold move, at least for me, I invited him to spend the night.

He said he wasn't sure what would happen if he stayed.

I thought his wording was odd. I knew exactly what would happen, considering I wore only panties, and his jeans were shoved down past his knees. I could still taste the cum from his orgasm on my tongue. I had no doubt about what would happen if he stayed.

Since he refused a sleepover, I reluctantly kicked him out at midnight. I needed sleep. I had a meeting scheduled in the morning and a busy day in the office.

After a lingering goodbye at the door, I watched him walk off into the night, swallowed quickly by the shadows as if he'd never been there at all.

It didn't take long before I started waiting for his rap at my door as each day drew to a close. After that first day, I gave my assistant, Gary, instructions to schedule meetings later in the morning.

He looked me up and down, noted the smile I was trying to hide under my professional demeanor, and grinned. "Uh Huh. Should I get an extra cushion for your desk chair for the days he fucks you tender?"

"Gary." I said in mock sternness, and then we both laughed.

45

"Boss Lady," his smile was genuine. "I'm just really glad you found someone."

Autumn turned into winter. My mystery man stopped in each day after work, and he'd shovel my walkway and do whatever minor tasks I needed help with around my house.

We'd spend the evenings cuddled together, watching television. Doing jigsaw puzzles became a contest of titillation and willpower until he'd bend me over the back of the sofa and plunge deeply into me until we were both breathless or I chased him up the stairs to have my wicked way with him. Then we'd chat until the wee hours until he had to leave.

It was hard not falling in love with him. But I knew better.

He left too much unsaid, gave vague answers to my questions about his family and avoided topics that would tell me about his personal life. Even though he was wonderful, and Dash adored him, he wasn't worth the risk to my heart.

If I let myself fall, I'd be devastated when he eventually left, and somehow, I knew he would leave. Still, that didn't stop me from taking him upstairs to my bedroom every night.

He was an attentive student, and my body was his favourite text. Each encounter was new and exciting as he licked and sucked on my pussy with reckless precision. His goal seemed to be to make me come harder and longer than the time before. He never asked for anything in return, but I worshipped his body, anyway.

I loved kissing my way down over his chest. He claimed he wasn't sensitive, but his nips tightened into tiny erections under the pressure of my tongue and when I applied the slightest suction, his eyes rolled back in his head. I'd trace the outline of his abs with my lips as I cradled his balls and stroked his cock until I was ready to swallow his head and tease around his swollen ridge.

Sometimes I'd leave my mouth open and slide him in and out. Other times I'd take him as far as I could to the back of my throat and flatten my tongue against his length until he jerked in reaction. Then I'd pull back to kiss the tip and run my tongue over his crown before plunging down over him again. My fingers never ceasing as they cupped his balls or played with his taint.

Sometimes, his orgasm hit so fast, I barely had a warning before he exploded into my mouth. He'd grunt out his release as it hit the back of my throat and apologize later for not giving me a heads up.

Personally, I took it as a compliment that I could make him lose control.

Each night, we seemed to try a new position or a technique. I'm sure my search history would raise eyebrows amongst my friends.

He definitely seemed to appreciate my efforts as I did his.

My only complaint was that he always left before I woke up.

I tried to wake in time to send him off, but he was stealthy. I never felt him get up, yet he always left a glass of juice on my nightstand with a tender message written in his strong script to tell me he'd be thinking of me.

Despite my best efforts, I was losing my heart to him. As the deepest part of the winter passed, I noticed he began arriving later and later in the evenings. Until finally, I saw the sadness in his eyes I'd been dreading.

"I have to leave tomorrow."

"Why?"

"I can't explain. Please, believe me. It's not my choice."

"Why didn't you tell me sooner? Give me a chance to prepare."

"You mean a chance to talk me out of it?" His smile was sad. "I hoped it would be different. It felt different, but fate can be a rigid master." His explanation made no sense.

I wanted to scream at him. Make him change his mind until I looked into his eyes and saw his devastation matched my own.

I still didn't understand anything except his pain was as great as mine.

In the morning, I woke at his kiss on my forehead and his whispered, "I love you." Heartbroken and unable to face his final goodbye, I was a coward and pretended to still be asleep.

He paused at the door and spoke softly. "I hoped love would have been enough. I don't want to go, but the choice isn't mine." He took a step and then hesitated once more. "I will always watch over you."

Needing one last look, I opened my eyes as he left my bedroom to see his head hung low and shoulders slumped.

The note he left on my bedside table said, "Until we meet again."

I heard my front door close and raced to the window to watch him walk away in the pre-dawn light. I'd never actually seen which direction he went when he left.

It must have been a trick of the light, because he seemed to disappear into the mist as the first rays of the sun crested the horizon.

Later that morning, I realized we'd changed to Daylight Savings Time overnight. That evening, to celebrate, I pulled out my patio furniture and propane firepit and watched the shadows come to life. It was a poor substitute for the company I'd enjoyed over the winter, but I'd promised myself I wouldn't wallow like I did the last time I'd been left alone in this house.

That evening, Dash sat faithfully by my side until I lit the fire to ward off the evening's chill.

Habit made me look over to see if I could see the silhouette of the man in the fedora with a cigarette hanging from his mouth, in the shadows.

There he was. He wasn't exactly the same as he was last fall because the once barren trees were filled with buds. Still, the sight of him made me smile.

At that same moment, my old dog raced to the stairs and headed for the lawn.

"Don't chase any deer," I told him. "And stay away from the road." I added when I remembered that night last fall when the man who stole my heart first arrived.

Dash trotted over to the feet of my imaginary man made of shadows, whimpering as if confused. My pet circled and sniffed around, finally lying down at the edge of the lawn. His chin rested on his paws in the same position he'd often taken at my beau's feet over winter.

"Looks like he's happy to see you again too, old friend," I said to the shadow. "So much has happened since I've last spoken to you." I sat down in my chair and only cried a little when I told the shadow about my wonderful winter companion.

I know. I know. It sounds crazy, but it was therapeutic.

The leaves grew on the trees, eventually obscuring the man's silhouette. Still, I spoke to him all summer, recapping my daily activities and reliving different memories from the time spent with my mysterious companion and my hope that we could be together again.

Spring changed to summer, which bled into fall.

Then it was too cold to sit out on the deck, even with the fire going. I let Dash out, expecting him to go curl up in his favorite spot at the edge of the lawn. Instead, he raced around the house at the same moment my doorbell rang.

Logic warred with an irrational hope that the man I'd lost had come back. Which made me angry too. Those thoughts fled when I opened my front door and was swept up into his arms.

"I've missed you so much." He whispered into my hair as he held me close.

Dash came in with him, acting like a puppy as he danced around our feet.

He didn't put me down until he'd walked us into the living room and sat on the couch with me in the familiar position of straddling his hips

I wanted to argue. I needed to demand an explanation.

How could he leave me alone for so long but when I met his eyes, I could see the same longing in his gaze as I'm sure was in mine. It hadn't been just a line. His absence hadn't been voluntary.

In that moment, I realized I had a choice to make.

I could waste our time together with questions and recriminations, or I could value each new moment with him. Which is what I chose to do. "I hated being away from you, but I'm so glad you're here now." Tomorrow I may regret my decision, but tonight I just needed him.

His shoulders sagged with relief as he gathered me close against him.

I breathed in his familiar, woodsy scent. I'd spent hours in the drugstore last spring trying to figure out what product he used so I could buy it. Probably not a healthy way to cope, but I'd been desperate.

Ultimately, it didn't matter, nothing came close to the real thing.

He kissed me hard, as if he couldn't get close enough to me. Then he pushed my hips away till I was teetering on the edge of his knees.

My heart broke until he stood up, gathering me in his arms again and headed for the stairs. "Please tell me this is okay." he begged, pausing at the bottom step.

"Get your ass up those stairs." I didn't hesitate. I'd face any consequences tomorrow, and I was okay with that.

Once upstairs, he tossed me on the bed and dove in after me, pressing me into the mattress.

His chest against mine and that delightful rod in his jeans wedged between my legs as I wrapped my ankles around his waist to pull him in tighter.

Like our very first night, we made out like teenagers. Reacquainting ourselves with the feel of each other's body. Clothes came off. His sweater and shirt, and then my jeans. When he stood to take off his pants, I ripped off my hoodie and sports bra, ignoring the sound of snapping threads.

My smile was mischievous as I reached over for the remote. I'd made a new addition to my bedroom. I clicked on the electric fireplace to ease the chill.

This time when his body covered mine, I could feel his delightfully hairy chest rub against my erect nipples and his cock already notched at my entrance.

I was soaked. At my nod, he pushed inside. I stretched around him as he pressed in all the way to the hilt.

He gave me a second to adjust before he pulled out and plunged in again.

My hips rose, meeting every thrust with one of my own.

It was fast. Furious strokes. Unbridled gasps.

He threw his head back and bellowed as he pulsed inside me. The tendons in his neck stood stark against the smoothness of his neck, and that's when I noticed it.

In the shadows cast by the fireplace, I realized the truth about who he was.

What he was.

It was there in the planes of his face as the firelight flickered over his features, casting shade in the shape of leaves and twigs.

He was my man, made of shadows, come to life.

Amelia Dax

EM-BODY-MENT

This morning started like any other.

My alarm sounded, and I rolled over to turn off the annoying upbeat music before the pre-programmed volume increase blared me into a bad mood.

Reluctantly, I swung my legs over the edge and pulled my slippers close enough to put on, so my feet didn't have to feel the shock of the cold floor after my warm bed. I wanted to hold on to those last tendrils of sleep for as long as I could. To help, I wrapped myself in my fluffy blue robe.

After a trip to the bathroom, I toddled out to the kitchen, grateful I'd remembered to load up the coffeemaker and set the start-timer. The machine was making its last wheezes when I walked through the doorway.

In seconds, I had a mug of fresh coffee cradled against my chest, trying to reclaim the cozy I'd left in my bed.

Two cups later, I felt ready to face the morning and poured myself a bowl of cereal. The grown-up kind, mostly. The box assured me it only had two grams of sugar. I didn't want to think about what artificial chemical they put inside to give it that sweet taste.

After breakfast, I opened my laptop and got to work. I had a few deadlines coming up and a video meeting later this morning.

Our company was about to invest in a smaller manufacturing venture that needed a capital injection to expand operations, as it was poised to make massive amounts of money.

My boss thought he was making a great deal, but I didn't trust the other company's CEO.

He seemed too slick.

There was already an email from Cindy, my boss's assistant. I poured myself another coffee and wished for something stronger to add to the dark brew before opening what I knew would be an over-the-top perky missive about streamers, candy and fake gravestones. She'd been asked to arrange the company's Halloween party and desperately wanted my input. I guess because we were the only two women in the office.

Saved by the bell. I thought as my doorbell chimed.

Still in my robe, I turned the knob to answer my door. I was expecting a new set of noise cancelling earphones to wear at the office. Cindy was even more bubbly and distracting in person and seemed to take the phrase "I'm busy" as an invitation to chat.

Anthony, the regular delivery driver, winked when he saw my outfit. "I keep telling you Georgia, I'm married." He handed me the package and waved over his shoulder as he headed back to his truck.

I looked at my fuzzy royal blue housecoat. "Aww, you don't think a woman dressed up like the cookie monster is sexy?" I teased his retreating back.

He turned around, smiling widely. "Of course. But I prefer Big Bird." And hopped up into his truck.

I closed my door, still smiling. We'd had that conversation dozens of times, and I still thought it hilarious. I met his husband once when I ran into them at the grocery store. His hubby still says hi every time we run into each other.

Once back in my house, I paused. Do I open that email from freakin' Cindy, or do I take my break early to try out my new headphones? I had an audiobook that was just getting to the good part when I stopped it before bed last night. I shut it down because there was no sense in getting myself all riled up before trying to go to sleep.

Then I remembered, new electronics usually came with just enough charge for testing. You had to plug them in for an hour or two before use.

Resigned to not being able to avoid the email from Cindy, I plugged them in.

To my surprise, the light was already a solid green, indicating the earphones were fully charged and ready to go. I grabbed them, my phone and my coffee and headed into the living room.

I sat down on my loveseat. Sideways, so I could tuck my feet under the cushion at the end and pulled my afghan over my legs.

Cozy was still the theme of the day.

I put them on so I could hear the audible instructions for syncing to my phone.

"Hello, Baby Girl. I am so very happy to be with you." The voice was deep. Its velvety smooth tone flowed into my ears and sent a tingle up my spine.

My head jerked in surprise. This was not the robotic voice I was expecting to give me instructions on how to connect to my phone. I wasn't about to complain.

"Well, hello to you too." I smiled and gave my shoulders a shake to ease the sudden tension his voice invoked, and then said to my empty room, "Mmmm, damn that voice is sexy."

"Why thank you."

"What …the!?" I ripped the headset off and tossed it to my feet. "What the hell was that?" I searched around my room and even looked out to the street to see if someone was pranking me.

At the other end of the loveseat, I could hear the rumbling of that deep voice. Carefully, as if afraid of setting off a bomb, I pick the headset back up. Holding it a safe distance from my face, just in case.

Just in case of what, I had no idea.

Slowly, I brought the headphones back up to my ears. I didn't actually put them on, I just held them close enough to hear what he was saying.

He must have sensed I was near somehow, because he was no longer shouting. "I'm sorry, Baby Girl," he said in a soothing voice, "I didn't mean to scare you. I should have known better, but frankly, I got excited when you put me on."

"But. But you're a set of headphones." I stated the obvious.

"Yes, Baby Girl. I am embodied in a set of headphones."

"Embodied?" I looked around, still trying to figure out who would play this type of joke on me. "Does this mean you're a ghost?"

"Honestly, I'm not sure," he said. "I think so, but I don't remember ever living. My first memory is of some guy who put me over his ears and fiddled with my buttons. I told him he shouldn't be touching me like that, but I don't think he understood what I was saying. He just verified I made noise and didn't bother listening to what I was saying. He was too busy talking to the person beside him. Then I was packed into a box and shipped to you."

"So now you just live in my headphones?"

"I think I am your headphones," he said as if he was considering this for the first time. "I felt your hands pick me up. I can hear you when you're holding me or even just close to me."

Cautiously, I put him back over my head, settling the noise cancelling foam comfortably around my ears.

He let out a soft groan. "This is the best I've ever felt," he whispered. "It feels like I've come home."

"So, what do I do? Do I treat you like my headphones and hook you up to my phone? Is it rude to treat you like just another gadget?"

"No, Baby Girl. I want to know everything about you. Hook me up to your playlists and your audiobooks. We can chat in between songs, or we can discuss the books you're listening to. I am here for you. Only you, in whatever way you need me."

I had to laugh because I knew what kind of books I read. "What if what I'm reading is naughty?"

"Then I will listen to it along with you, and we will both be aroused."

One of my friend's husbands liked reading her smutty books. She said it doubled the excitement between them both inside and outside of the bedroom. Truly, the thought of the person/entity in my headphones listening to the audiobook along with me amped up the titillation. I opened the settings on my phone and connected the headset.

I half expected him to say something cheesy like, "Oh baby, that feels good." when the devices connected. But he didn't say or do anything to make it feel weird, or more weird than it already did.

I wavered a bit before I dove right back into the book I was listening to about high school sweethearts reconnecting after decades apart. They'd been making out on the couch when I shut it down before bed. "I don't think

I'm ready to jump into the sexy stuff with you. I know it sounds silly, but we just met."

"That's okay, Baby Girl," his low voice responded, sending a chill down my spine in the best possible way. "We can start slow, test your limits and mine. Learn how I respond to you because I'm not really sure what my capabilities are." He paused. "I know that I can feel the warmth of your head and the silkiness of your hair caressing over the top of my foam pads surrounding your ears, and I love the way you touch my buttons."

That made me laugh because it was such a ridiculous statement, yet sexy and slightly creepy all at the same time. Not sleezy-creepy, but haunted-creepy. "Okay," I said. "Let's start off slow while we figure this out." I got up and walked to the kitchen for another cup of coffee. I glanced at the clock and still had an hour before my video meeting. Realizing I had plenty of time, I opened my phone and chose one of my favourite songs. A remake of The Sound Of Silence, by Disturbed.

As I refilled my cup, I hummed along with the vocal. I love David Draiman's voice. It was so rich and had such texture to it.

About halfway through the song, another voice started humming along with me. It sang the same low notes but had a much different tone. It was more mellow and didn't have the gravel raspiness of David's voice.

I paused the song. "Is that you singing along? If you are brand new, how do you even know the words?"

"I guess we both just discovered something about me."

"That's kind of cool. I think." I took a sip of my coffee and pondered. Was he a fast learner, or was there something more sinister happening?

I restarted the song. This time, I stayed silent while he sang along. When it finished, I searched on my phone for another song to play. I chose I Hope You Dance by Lee Ann Womack. I'd always loved that song. Not wanting to think about the implications of my headset's ability to know things, I set my coffee cup back on the counter and swayed to the music. I closed my eyes and crossed my arms across my chest to hug myself. I moved my hips to the beat until I felt a warm sensation at my back. Then someone took my hand and pulled me out into a spin.

My eyes flew open and the hand holding mine disappeared. I stumbled when I realized there was no one in front of me and my momentum carried me forward until I caught myself on the kitchen island.

"What the fuck?!" I asked the empty room.

"I'm sorry, Baby Girl. I didn't realize it was actually happening. I imagined I was dancing with you and then your hand was in mine and I got a little carried away."

I braced my hands against the kitchen counter while my knees trembled. "How can you hold my hand? You are a set of earphones."

"I don't know, darling. I have no explanation. I just know when I pictured myself reaching out to hold your hand, I did."

"Forgive me for stating the obvious," I said, "but you are a headset. You don't have eyes."

"Apparently, my love, I have a very good imagination." His chuckle was low, then trailed off to a more serious note. "I don't have a mouth either, but you can hear me. I don't know how this is possible, but I'm so glad it is."

"Did I fall and bang my head?" I questioned aloud. "There has got to be some explanation."

"I agree." The voice in my ear said. "If there is, I have no idea what it could be. I seem to be like Alexa, the AI assistant. I'm able to access the internet and all its knowledge, yet I can't find a single reference to anything like this. Like me."

That niggling fear came back to the forefront of my thoughts. "You're not going to hurt me or take over my body in an attempt to rule the world, are you?"

His laugh echoed through the speakers. "Baby Girl. I'd cut out my battery pack if I thought I was going to cause you harm."

I hadn't noticed he'd muted the music while we spoke until the instrumental bridge in the song increased in volume.

"Shall we try that spin again?" He asked.

I adjusted the headphones on my head where they'd been knocked slightly askew in my near tumble. I took another sip of coffee, a deep breath, and then closed my eyes. Giving myself over to the moment. "Sure, let's try this again."

One song bled into another as we waltzed across the floor. For someone with no body, he was an incredibly good dancer. He led me around the kitchen with the touch of his hand at my elbow, or at the small of my back. The next time he spun me, I kept hold of his hand and he pulled me back against him. My back to his front.

I leaned my head into his shoulder and sighed. "You're the perfect height."

"I was made just for you." He whispered in my ear.

He'd even nailed my taste in music.

Somehow, he must have heard my thoughts, because he chuckled, "I have access to your playlists, and I picked out songs that seemed to fit the moment."

"Too bad you weren't real. You'd be the perfect boyfriend." Horrified, I realized what I'd said. "I don't mean that you aren't real, just…"

There was sadness in his voice. "I know, Baby Girl. I know exactly what you mean, but as long as I can feel you against me. I'm content."

We danced and swayed to the music until my alarm went off, warning me I had ten minutes before I had to open the online meeting. I carefully set him on the vanity while I brushed my hair and teeth and slapped on some makeup.

On my way back to the kitchen, I threw a blazer on over my tank top and logged in to open the meeting room. While I waited for the other attendees to arrive, I synced my headset to my laptop in case I wanted to use it later.

The meeting was to go over the final items about our investment in that smaller company.

Their CEO was always a smarmy asshole, and I honestly didn't trust him, but my boss thought that he wasn't stupid enough to misrepresent their company and pushed to go ahead.

I put my new headset on the counter beside my laptop. I didn't want to be distracted during the meeting. Shortly after my boss began talking, I heard a hissing sound. I put myself on mute so that the noise wouldn't carry through to the meeting and looked around for the source.

"Baby Girl, you cannot buy that company." His voice sounded tinny because I was too far away from the headset and he had turned himself up to full volume.

"What do you mean?" I said through closed lips so that no one would know I was talking to someone else while in the meeting.

"Remember how I said I was like Alexa, and could access the internet? Well, since we're on an open port through the zoom meeting and this guy's got shit for security, I can access his files. Their warehouse is about to be condemned. He falsified the inspection reports, which means that you're about to make a bad deal. Tell them you insist on getting another inspection with an inspector you can trust who will report directly to you."

"You're sure?" I asked. "You're not like those AI programs that just collect random information and try to pull it together."

"No Baby Girl, I have a sentient mind. I can think for myself I can see the pictures of mold in the basement and the real, un-doctored inspection report in a secure folder on his desktop. Here, look."

I glanced at my computer screen as images appeared one after another, and the slimy CEO's face looked suspiciously more smug than usual. I decided to trust the headphones and ask for a delay before committing to the investment.

God, I'd have to get him a name. I can't just keep calling him 'headphones'. I thought as I unmuted my microphone.

"Gentlemen, sorry to interrupt." My voice firm. "I know you have provided an inspection report, but I would like to pause this investment process until we can send our own inspectors out to look at the building. I've had some information delivered to me from a trusted source, which would be remiss of me to ignore. I'd like to verify before we go any further in the process."

My boss looked shocked.

I met his stare through the screen and texted 'trust me' to him on my phone.

He nodded. "Very well. We will pause this until an additional inspection can be done. It would be in everybody's best interest if it could be completed later today, or tomorrow."

I shifted my gaze to the other man to gauge his reaction to my delay. "It depends on the inspector's schedule. I'll send you over the details of when to expect them, and then we'll reconvene once the reports are verified." Then I told both men. "Everything else is in place and it should be smooth sailing from there."

My boss left, but I didn't closeout the meeting immediately. As always, the meetings were recorded, and I was curious if the CEO would forget that little detail and slip up. He always treated me like a secretary instead of the second in command. Would he say something incriminating to me now that my boss was no longer in the meeting?

The man on the other side of my screen's expression was furious. "You little bitch, what game are you playing?"

I looked him dead in the eye through the monitor and nodded to myself.

His angry reaction told me everything I needed to know.

The headphones were right.

I didn't answer him, I just ended the meeting.

My boss called me on the phone an instant later. "What the hell was that? What's going on?"

"While we were in the meeting, I received word that he falsified the inspection report. Specifically, there's mold coming up in through the basement between the walls. Also, additions were made that aren't even close to the safety code, creating a fire hazard that will be impossible to fix without replacing the whole electrical system. The facility we're about to invest in is beyond repair, let alone able to be upgraded."

"You're sure about this?"

"Franklin, when have I ever steered you wrong?"

My boss sighed. "Yeah, you're right. If you trust your source, do a thorough investigation."

"Thank you, Franklin."

Later, once the post-meeting furor calmed down, and I was ready to break for lunch, my mind drifted back to what I should call my new friend as I put him back on my head and adjusted his foam pads around my ears.

I purposefully didn't put him on after my meeting. He would have been a distraction I wouldn't have been able to resist. I would have chatted with him instead of working.

"What should I call you?" I asked in greeting.

"You don't need to call me, Baby Girl. I'm always right here."

That made me laugh. "Not call like on the phone, I mean as a name. You always call me Baby Girl."

"Oh." The concept seemed to surprise him. "I suppose I could have a name. But if you asked a friend to hand you Charles, they wouldn't know you meant your headphones and it would be hard to explain."

"True. But when I'm referring to you in my head, I want to call you by name, not just my headphones."

"Fair." He paused. "And I appreciate you not thinking about me as an object."

"How about HP?" I asked him. "It's not very original but…."

"It's perfect." He interrupted. "Everything is an acronym these days."

"I have an hour before I need to log back in. I usually read over lunch. Are you sure you want to listen to the book I was reading? It's rather spicy."

He laughed and said, "Well, I may have been born yesterday, at least that's what I feel like. But I'm not a child. Who knows? Maybe listening together will enhance the experience."

My laugh caught in my throat. I could already feel my face redden with just the hope of his sexy voice replacing the narrator. The thought of his voice reverberating through my body as if he was in fact whispering sweet nothings directly in my ear while lying beside me. Aside from a couple of my female friends with similar tastes, most people didn't even know that I read anything but business books. I'm pretty straightlaced in real life. "I have never listened to these books with anyone before."

"Then I am honoured to be your first," his voice rumbled. "Shall we pick up where you left off?"

"Absolutely." I said, eager for the experience now that I'd overcome my shyness and the shock of having my headset have a mind of its own. As I hoped, he read the book to me.

I led her to the bedroom. I've wanted this woman since the first moment I saw her, and now I was about to have her. My cock stood at high mast, pushing against the stiffness of my jeans, every step equally painful and exciting.

I wanted to undo my pants and relieve some of the tension, but I didn't want to take my hands from hers as I stepped backwards, guiding her down the hall toward my bedroom.

Her eyes never left mine, not even to look around my personal space as we entered the room.

I stopped when the back of my legs hit the mattress, leaving it up to her to make the next step.

She'd break me if she called it off, but I wasn't about to let her feel forced.

My heart stopped when she let go of my hands, restarting only when she grasped the hem of her flowy t-shirt and pulled it up over her head.

Her body was the stuff of fantasies. Her breasts, round globes that hung heavy in her lace bra with her nipples poking at the see-through fabric.

I couldn't help myself. I reached forward and cradled her heavy mounds in my hands as my thumb stroked over their tips.

I gasped. "I felt that." Just like in the kitchen, there was no one touching me, but I felt the warmth of hands holding my breasts, and my nipples were so hard. As if someone had actually been playing with them.

I could hear his deep chuckle in my ears. "I hoped that would happen. After our dance in the kitchen this morning, I had been eagerly waiting to try this."

"So, you mean every time I read a book, I'm going to feel you?"

"I think so. He sounded positively gleeful. I don't know if I can explain it," he said. "I don't have any knowledge prior to us meeting, but this feels like it's the way it's supposed to be."

"What if I read a murder mystery or listen to the news?" My concern was genuine. "I listen to everything on my phone. If they describe a murder, are you going to kill me?" It seemed a valid question.

I could hear his indrawn breath. "No. No, absolutely not," he said. "It would kill me to cause you harm." Then he chuckled. "I am here for your listening pleasure, with the huge emphasis on pleasure."

"Can we test it? Will you switch to the news?" I hated not trusting his words, but did he actually know? This was as new to him as it was to me. My hands were on the headset to whip it off and break our connection, just in case.

He might have been born yesterday, but I wasn't. Not that I could ever have anticipated having the ability to dance or become intimate with a set of headphones.

He switched himself over to the news. In fact, he switched himself to several different news stations, one after another, to make sure he got a broadcast that was talking about war and murder. He even took over the broadcast himself, using his voice to give the news. To prove that even though some of these heinous deeds were described in his voice, I was still safe.

He even switched over to read the most gruesome murder scene told from the point of view of the killer.

I don't even know what book that was, and I hope I never read it. It was sadistic in the worse way, but aside from chills down my spine, and the hair rising on my arms, I felt nothing from him, except for the warmth of a hug after he finished.

And while I recognized maybe he could just turn it on and off at will, he managed to ease the worst of my fears. I reminded myself, even when he read the sexy bits and I felt his touch, I hadn't felt incapacitated, and his touch disappeared when I opened my eyes.

"Shall we continue he asked, and I nodded as if he could see me. He started speaking as if he felt my nod and understood.

Good to know. I filed that piece of information away for future reference as we explored his capabilities and what was happening between us.

I slid my arms around her and pulled her close. Pressing her delicious breasts against my chest as I made short work of the clasp of her bra.

"I love the feel of you against me." I sighed, keeping my eyes closed as I explored his body. "Do you know you have the perfect amount of hair on your chest?" I moved my hands up over his shoulders and then down his arms to get an idea of his size. I'd felt him against me before when we were dancing. But this time I explored him slowly, gliding my hands over his shoulders up his neck, trying to get an idea of what he looked like from the shape of his face.

He had a strong jaw, hair that seemed to curl slightly over his ears, and a wide smile.

This time, it was his turn to suck in his breath. I'm not sure how you did that, but don't stop.

"I won't, but hang on a sec. We're taking a field trip."

I opened my eyes and raced down the hall to my bedroom and laid down on the bed. I don't even remember taking my work blazer off, although I vaguely remember tossing it toward the couch.

As soon as I put my head on the pillow, he said, "Now where were we?"

"I followed her down to the mattress, my knees between her legs and my hands on either side of her shoulders to hold me up so I could just stare at her beauty. She was really here. In my bed. My personal fantasy had come to life."

"She reached up and stroked my cheek, winding her fingers in the hair at the back of my neck. She pulled me

down toward her. I followed her lead. Willing to go wherever she took me. She raised her head to close the distance between our lips."

I did exactly that. I reached up and wrapped my hands around his neck and brought his mouth to mine. There was no tentativeness when we touched. Need overtook us as our lips came together. Demanding. Feral. I breathed him in until he was a part of me.

We'd gone from reading the book to acting it out.

When he broke our kiss, he continued. Mimicking the movements of the novel as he whispered the words in my ear.

"I pulled back to give her space, but she pulled me down to her. One hand still gripped my hair, the other around my torso, pulling me against her. I adjusted my weight, lowering myself to my elbows. My body skimmed over hers as she arched her back, pressing her breasts into my body. I shifted my hips, dragging my erection over the wet cloth between her legs. I almost came on the spot. It felt like the seams in my jeans were going to burst from the tautness of the fabric."

"Oh, God." I moaned as I squeezed my eyes closed and dug my heels into my mattress. My knees spread wide as I forced my hips up to rub against him. Stupid me. I'd left my panties on, but I didn't want to stop to take them off. The feeling was too delicious, and the rumble of his deep voice in my ear intensified the effect.

I trailed kisses down the edge of her lips, then along her jaw. I nestled for a few seconds in the crook of her neck. Licking and nipping, never breaking the rhythm of gently rubbing my body against hers until I moved lower. The tips of her breasts, now free from her bra, rose up to meet me as if eager for my touch.

I felt every whisper from his lips against my skin. I didn't know how he'd undone my bra, and right now, I didn't care. All I knew was that my body had never felt so alive before.

His words echoed in my ears as gooseflesh raised along my skin where his nonexistent body touched mine, following the author's directions in ways I could never have imagined.

Then his mouth was on me. Licking me through the nearly sheer fabric. Applying pressure just where I needed it. I felt his fingers trail up the inside of my thighs until they reached the juncture and gently pulled the fabric away, exposing me to him.

He moved his head away only far enough to remove the barrier of fabric. Then he was back. His thumbs moving the protective swell of my labia away to give him better access.

I wondered if he'd researched how to go down on a woman with that big internet access brain of his because his tongue moved in ways I'd never dreamed of.

My breath came in gasps as each flick of his tongue sent shockwaves of pleasure through me. My legs tightened around his head, to both hold him in place and protect myself from his onslaught. The sensations were so intense. It didn't take long until the heavy feeling between my legs grew, and my muscles clenched, preparing me to ride out what I knew was going to be the most exquisite orgasm of my life.

He read me like a book. Responding to every moan and quiver until he triggered my orgasm.

A kaleidoscope of bright white light exploded behind my eyes as I thrust myself up against his mouth. His hands seemed to be everywhere, in ways not possible by a mere mortal man. He gripped my ass as he pressed his hair-roughened chest against my breasts and sucked on my nipples without his mouth leaving my clit.

He surrounded me with sensation until I felt I was levitating off the bed with pleasure as my orgasm flowed between us like a living thing. Wave after wave washed over me, as he coaxed more from me than I had ever given before. Each time I thought my orgasm was receding, he adjusted his touch to prolong the intensity. He was going to kill me, after all.

Finally, he sensed when I could take no more and he gently brought me back to earth. Easing his ministrations to allow my overstimulated nerves to settle.

Eventually, my euphoria turned to a languid relaxation. My body felt heavy against the bed as I felt him stretch out beside me.

"I learned online that a woman's orgasm could last for several minutes." he chuckled. "I'd ask how I did, but I think I already know."

"Good." I murmured sleepily. "So very good." I smiled as he leaned over to brush the hair from my forehead. "So, Mr. Smarty-pants. How long did you make my orgasm last? Did you break the world record?"

"Not this time. They say it's best to work our way up and build your endurance. This one lasted only seventy-two seconds. I'll do better next time."

"That's a plan I can get behind." I giggled softly. "I think I need a nap before going back to work this afternoon."

"Geez and I haven't even fucked you yet." He didn't sound offended at all. In fact, he still sounded rather pleased with himself.

"I'm sorry." I stammered. "We should look after you."

"No, Baby Girl." His voice was gentle but firm. "We have all the time in the world. You rest for a while. In fact, let me sing you a lullaby and I'll wake you in time to go back to work."

The last thing I heard was his deep velvet voice as I drifted off to dreamland.

Amelia Dax

BEWITCHED DILDO

My ex is a witch. Not a bitch or a horrible person. She's a witch, which I wish I understood better when she warned me.

I just thought she was being self-deprecating. Letting me know that she might have a temper or be the jealous sort.

Nope, she was a practicing witch.

I call her my ex, but even that is a misnomer. She is my captor. My jailor. The person in charge of what's left of my existence. It's both a blessing and a curse.

I guess I should start at the beginning.

We met online last year on one of those dating sites. We chatted for a few days before meeting for a coffee at a cute little bookstore café. We'd hit it off immediately. Coffee turned into dinner, which turned into breakfast the next morning.

It's not like that. We didn't have sex that first night. We fell asleep on her couch talking until the wee hours of the morning.

I woke up and just stared at her. Completely smitten. I knew she was the one I wanted to wake up to for the rest of my life.

She eventually woke. A smile bloomed across her face when she saw I was still there. She told me later how she liked that I didn't try to take advantage of her that first night. Said it spoke volumes about what type of guy I was.

We were inseparable after that.

I'd been trying to be a gentleman.

By the time we'd had our fourth date, her frustration was palpable. "Don't you want me?" she'd asked.

Confused because I pulled back once again despite my obvious arousal after kissing her goodbye.

"I want you for more than just sex." I reassured her.

"What if that's all I want you for?" She teased.

At least I thought she was just teasing. Looking back now, I understand how important physical intimacy was to her.

She tugged the belt at the waistband of my jeans and pulled me toward her and guided me into the house.

I kicked the door closed behind me and pushed her up against the wall in her foyer and pressed my body against hers. This time, when our lips met, it wasn't a chaste goodnight kiss. I held nothing back, putting all my pent-up passion in the way I took her mouth under mine.

She tasted of coffee and the ice cream we'd stopped for on the way home and I couldn't get enough. She must have felt the same way because she rose to her toes and wrapped her arms around my shoulders, bringing me even closer.

I bent my knees to slide my palms down over her hips and under her thighs. "Hang on." I warned, as I lifted her from the floor.

She understood the assignment as she wrapped her legs around my waist. "Bedroom." She ordered without letting her mouth leave mine. She didn't need to tell me twice.

Already familiar with her home after that first night, I strode past her living room and down the hall. Careful to make sure I didn't bang either of us into the doorframe as I entered her bedroom.

My brain raced, trying to decide which of my fantasies about this moment I'd make a reality first. With her legs coiled around me so tightly, I knew I'd break her ankle if I fell to the bed and let her land on top of me. So, I fell forward. Letting her fall to the mattress while I caught my weight above her, without breaking our kiss.

Her fingers immediately started tearing at the buttons of my dress shirt and then hauled it out of the waistband of my jeans.

I stood up to strip my shirt and undershirt off while she sat up and started working on my pants. I'd already kicked off my shoes by the time she pushed my waistband down my hips far enough to haul my rock-hard cock out and swallow it.

She took me almost all the way to the root.

My knees buckled and would have toppled if she hadn't had such a firm grip on my ass. "Fuck, Babe." I grit my teeth to keep from cumming like a preteen. "Your mouth is amazing."

She didn't let up. Her hot, wet mouth surrounded me. Her tongue applying the perfect pressure to make my toes curl and my ass clench as I desperately tried to delay my orgasm even as it tightened my balls and rushed up into her mouth.

She barely backed off as my release exploded past her lips. It kept coming. Wave after wave emptied into her waiting mouth as she drank me down.

I dropped to the mattress beside her and rolled onto my back. My legs, unable to support my weight anymore. Several minutes passed before I had enough strength to open my eyes.

She lay alongside me, jean covered leg draped over my leg while her fingers played with the hair on my chest.

How the hell was she still dressed?

I thought back and realized aside from carrying her into the bedroom, I hadn't touched her at all. "I'm sorry. I'm such an asshole."

"Why do you think you're an asshole?" her voice was soft. Soothing.

"You still have your clothes on. I didn't even try to pleasure you before I came." I draped my forearm over my forehead and closed my eyes again. "That was a dick move."

"It's not like I gave you much choice." Her voice still held laughter, which made me feel only marginally better.

"I know." I risked a look sideways at her, and her expression reassured me. "It's just... I'm not that guy. The one who takes and doesn't make sure my partner is satisfied."

"I know you aren't." her tone was matter of fact. "If you were, I wouldn't have gone out with you a second time and you definitely wouldn't be lying naked on my bed right now."

That made me feel a little better. To show my appreciation, I lifted her blouse and rain kisses over her tummy while I worked the button and zipper of her jeans. Pulling the waistband away from her skin to trail my tongue over the freshly exposed flesh until she was squirming under my touch.

"Lift up." I whispered as I tugged the material down over her hips as I stood up to more easily pull the jeans from her legs and tossed them aside. I left her lace panties on, though.

Red lace had always been my favourite, which she knew from a previous conversation, so I wanted to show my appreciation for her thoughtfulness. I placed her legs back on the mattress, one on either side of me, as I eased my shoulders between her thighs.

I smiled as I watched the damp spot appear in the tiny slip of fabric. I hadn't even touched her yet. At least, not where it counted. I lowered my face and inhaled slowly as I brushed my nose up one side of the fabric and down the other. I did it again because her scent was intoxicating.

I wanted to rip her panties from her body and dive in, but she deserved more than that. So, I kissed and licked my way up the centre of her seam and then used my thumbs to spread her outer lips. Exposing her sensitive flesh, still covered in wet fabric. I took my time with her, alternating between licking on top of the fabric and lifting the edge to delve underneath.

Her hands grabbed at the sheets as she raised her hips, trying to force me to add more pressure. To stop teasing and give her an orgasm.

She was so close, I could taste it.

Satisfied she was ready, I grabbed one side of her waistband with both hands and ripped it apart, and then did the same to the other side. "I'll buy you another pair."

She gasped as I dove face first where we both needed me to be.

I dined like a starving man. Straightening my tongue and delving into her entrance while I used my nose to apply pressure to her clit.

If I suffocated, I'd die happy.

Then I flattened my tongue and took a long lick from inside her channel, up through her folds to suck on her tight little bundle of nerves.

Her hips alternated between thrusting up into my mouth and trying to escape because it was too much stimulation.

Amelia Dax

I rubbed my cock against the side of the mattress to give myself some relief from the ache in my balls while my hands held her hips firmly in place. I felt her entire body spasm as her orgasm crashed through her.

I didn't stop. I kept on that steady sucking until she jerked her hips out of my hands and pushed the top of my head away. "Enough." she said with a gasp.

I gave her the space she needed and just rested my forehead on her abdomen while she recovered. I didn't want to over stimulate her. I wasn't done yet.

Once her breathing was under control, I slid up her body. Kissing the underside of her breasts, around to their peaks, and then to her jaw. When our lips finally met, she sighed into my mouth and wrapped her arms around me. Bracing my body weight in one arm, I used the other hand to nudge my cock between her legs and slid it up and down her wetness to make sure I was well lubricated.

"Are you sure this is what you want?" I asked.

"Fuck me now." she growled and thrust her hips up.

I had no place to go but inside her. That first sweet slide was almost enough to make me come again.

She was so hot, slick, and tight. It took all my energy not to erupt before I made it all the way in.

I lowered my forehead to hers. I paused, enjoying the sensation of her muscles expanding and contracting around me, getting used to my girth. At her nod, I pulled out and slowly slid back in again and again.

Never had I felt such a detailed sensation. The way she gripped me. The smoothness of her thighs on the outside of my legs. The feel of her calves against my back as she looped her ankles together to hold me in place.

Not that I was going anywhere.

"Oh God." she moaned. Meeting each thrust, then holding me in place for an instant before letting me slide back out. She met my next thrust and the one after that. Occasionally, she squeezed her legs to hold me still while she rubbed herself against me.

I didn't mind.

Every time her muscles shifted around me, making it harder and harder to delay the inevitable orgasm.

"I have to move, babe." I warned her, no longer able to control the speed of my thrusts. They got faster, sharper, felt deeper and shallower all at the same time as my balls tightened up, warning me of the impending explosion. "I've got to pull out. I'm gonna come." I warned her.

"Don't. You. Dare." She hissed. "I'm on the pill." she explained, and then took control. In an instant she was on top of me, grinding down in an erratic figure eight motion, grinding her clit into my pubic bone.

It was all I could do to hang on to her ass and pray. She gave me no space to move, instead she used me like a sex toy.

I couldn't pull out without pushing her away.

She rose above me like a goddess. Her heavy breasts swayed in a mesmerizing pattern as she bounced on top of me. Then she suddenly bore down and froze. Her clit pressed against me, her inner muscles gripped me, and she threw her head back. The vibrations from her guttural scream echoed down through her channel and squeezed my cock.

The force of my orgasm took me by surprise. I half expected to see my cum shooting from her mouth from the force. Anything seemed possible.

"Holy shit," she said as she sagged down over me and her head nestled in the crook between my neck and shoulder. Her chest against mine and my cock still half hard inside her.

I wrapped my arms around her waist and turned us to the side. Disappointed when my cock slid out, but content to have her in my arms.

Two months later, I gave up the lease of my apartment and I moved into her house. It wasn't like I was spending much time at my place, anyway. She had a house and while the commute was a little longer, it was worth it for the ability to watch sunsets from her deck away from the noise of the city.

That's the polite reason. The real reason is I would follow that woman anywhere. Her pussy was magic. That first time we had sex, I thought I was going to expire from rapture. As we became familiar with each other's bodies and preferences, it had only gotten better. We'd even started to experiment. I loved every minute.

One day at work, one of my buddies brought in a big shopping bag and looked oddly self-conscious about it. He ducked into my office on the way to his own and said, "Hey can you come see me for a minute?"

Curious, I followed him down the hall.

"I bought a gift for my wife, and I have to get rid of it," he said with an embarrassed laugh. "It's not exactly something you can put up for grabs in the lunchroom."

Now I was really intrigued. "What on earth could you have bought for Jackie that she didn't like?" His wife had the best sense of humour.

"Well, apparently, I crossed a line with this one. I'm not even sure why because we saw it and she said it looked like it could be fun. But then she got upset when I showed up with it."

"What is it?" I asked, more curious than patient at this point.

He pulled out a cast making kit. Specifically designed to make a silicone model of a penis.

I burst out laughing because, as awesome as his wife was, she still went to church every Sunday. There was no way she was going to have any part of that. "Dude. What were you thinking?" I asked him.

He threw up his hands. "I know. I know. It was a silly idea, but she said it looked like fun. So, I got it for her."

"What do you think?" he asked me. "I need to get rid of it, and you were the first person I thought of. You're always walking around here with a smile on your face since you and your girl got together. Do you think she'd like it?"

I laughed. "Sure, I'll take it home to see if she wants to play."

My girlfriend thought it was hysterical.

After supper that night, she was scrolling on her phone while we listened to the news and she burst out laughing and showed me what was on her screen. Apparently, she was curious to see how much this kit would cost and saw it came with accessories.

You could buy an attachment to insert into the silicone as it was hardening, to provide various vibrations just like a real dildo. It was just a thin bar that looked like a meat thermometer with a remote control to switch vibration patterns.

"Order it." I told her. "If we're going to do this, let's do it right."

After the accessory package arrived, we prepared the gelatin like solution used to create the mould. While I mixed it in the container, she got down on her knees and took me into her mouth to get me nice and hard. Not that she had to do much. Just the thought of her playing with a dildo shaped like me had my cock at full mast.

The instructions warned that the gelatin hardened quickly. As soon as it started to thicken, she ducked out of the way, and I plunged my cock into the wide tube until it engulfed up to my balls. Even though the solution was warm and thick, it didn't take me long to lose my erection without her lips around me.

I'll admit, for the first time, I questioned my sanity for doing this. What if the finished product wasn't going to look as big as I thought I was?

I pulled myself away from the mouth of the wide tube while she poured in the silicone mixture and then added the thin straight bar for the vibrating component.

Once everything was done, we placed the container in the stand as instructed and left it on the counter to harden. It would take about forty-eight hours.

For the rest of the night, every time she and I looked at each other, we'd burst out laughing. It was such a ridiculous thing to do.

Two days later, we pulled the gel away from the silicone model of my cock. It wasn't as easy as the video instructions implied. She gave up and left me to continue to remove the bright green gel. I hated every minute of handling that fake cock, even though it was shaped like my own.

Eventually, there it was in all my glory. Which let us to even more laughter.

That night, she laid on her side facing me with my real cock in her mouth. She reached underneath the pillow. She pulled out our new silicon play toy and held it up against my dick and said, "Oh. I've never had twins before."

"I'll show you twins." I tapped my cock against her bottom lip until she opened her mouth again. Then I took the toy from her and pressed the button at the bottom.

It immediately sprang to life. I didn't bother asking her where the remote was. I knew I could control the pace with the buttons. I pushed her legs open and used my fingers to spread her nether lips, then teased her opening with my silicone twin.

She was already soaked, which I took full advantage of. I slid the toy between her legs, making sure to get it slicked up before I notched it at her entrance. Letting it just rest for a moment, vibrating steadily, until she shifted her hips to push it inside.

Her hand came back to my cock, jerking me off in a slow motion to encourage me to start moving the toy cock between her legs.

I took pity on her and eased it in and out gently and then more firmly as she moved against me and I readjusted to give her room to swallow me again. "There, now you've got me in both ends at the same time."

"So good." She murmured around my width.

"Maybe we should make another one for your asshole?" I told her, only half joking.

"Aflo-upp-we"

"Absolutely, eh?" I'll find out where he bought it and get another.

I tossed the toy aside and covered her with my body. Replacing the silicone with its living, ready to explode, twin.

"It's good, but you're so much better." She wrapped her legs around my waist, giving me more access to drive into her. "I need you forever." She gasped the instant before she tensed, grinding her clit against me.

"Forever." I promised after I came inside her and then kissed her forehead before collapsing on the bed, holding her close.

Two days later, I had lunch with my sister. She was in town for a couple of meetings and wanted to know if I could grab a bite for lunch with her. I barely recognized her when she approached my table.

Instead of having long flowing blonde hair like she'd worn for years. Her hair was cropped short in a pixie cut and she'd dyed it brown.

I knew she and her boyfriend had broken up recently, but I wasn't expecting such a drastic change. Even though we'd been close growing up, I didn't recognize her until she was standing at my table, looking down at where I sat with the telltale smirk on her face.

I insisted we take a selfie so that I could show my girlfriend when I got home. I knew she had meetings all day on the other side of town, so I hadn't invited her.

My sister was disappointed at the absence, but she understood.

That night when I got home, my girlfriend was quiet. Something was wrong, so in my efforts to find out what was bothering her, I completely forgot about seeing my sister.

Which was too bad. In hindsight, that photo of the two of us would have cheered her right up and not changed the course of the rest of our lives.

Well, my life.

You can imagine my surprise when I woke in the morning to nothing. I felt unsteady, as if I was being rolled gently from side to side. As if I was on a rowboat in the middle of the ocean.

I knew I was awake, but I felt like I was in a container of some sort. I could feel the breeze from the air conditioner blow freely over my body and it felt like my girlfriend's arm was around my middle. But it didn't feel like my body, and it didn't feel like her arm.

The air didn't ruffle the hair on my chest. I couldn't move my arms or legs, and it felt like her arm was the thing rolling me from side to side.

Like a bored person uses their finger to play with a pencil on their desk.

Then I realized I wasn't breathing. I couldn't feel air fill my lungs or exhale again. I paused, trying not to panic. Wait, a minute. "Where the fuck was my heartbeat?"

"Ah, so you're awake." She said from somewhere to my left. Her tone was quiet, almost modest. A far cry from the hedonistic screams she let out last night as I did everything I could to bring her out of her funk.

"What happened? Why can't I feel anything? Why is it so dark?"

"I sensed you were drifting away from me."

"Drifting away from you? What are you talking about?" I responded. Only now realizing I wasn't actually speaking. "What's going on?" this time I didn't try to hide my panic.

"I saw you with her." She replied. "I went to surprise you for lunch yesterday and I saw you with her. You were so familiar with each other. Laughing and joking and then you put your arm around her and snapped a selfie together.

I'd never heard her so angry.

But now I was too. "That was my sister. Go get my phone and look." I demanded. "You were supposed to be in meetings all day, so I didn't ask you to come to our last-minute lunch date. We took a selfie because she wanted to show you her new haircut. She did a post break up makeover and wanted you to see the result. I meant to show you when I got home, but you were upset and I forgot all about our lunch and was more concerned about you."

"Oh. That will teach me for jumping to conclusions." Her laugh was sad. "What's done is done."

"What do you mean, what's done is done? You didn't answer me. Why can't I feel my body?"

"It was destroyed during the last phase of the bonding ceremony." Her voice was only mildly regretful.

"What binding ceremony?" I screamed.

"Oh, calm down." This time, she seemed amused at my reaction. "I was afraid you were going to leave me, and I didn't want to live without you."

"What. Did. You. Do?"

"Remember that mould of your penis?"

"Yes. It was fun, but what's that got to do with anything?"

"Well, when I thought you were going to leave me, I bound your spirit to the silicone penis. So now I can have you forever."

She said it so matter-of-factly as if it was nothing. As if it was no big deal that she just destroyed my life.

"My life. My mom. What's going to happen to my mom?" My thoughts whirled in my head. "I was the only family she had left. Who would take her grocery shopping? Who would look after her if she gets sick?"

"Don't worry, I talked to your mother this morning. We're going out shopping later and I'll let her know that you were called away for work. While you're away, I'll tell her there was a nasty accident where they couldn't recover your body." I could hear the smile in her voice. "You know I love your mom. I'll look after her like my own."

"This can't be happening. Oh my God, this can't be happening." I tried to move my arms and legs. Nothing. I tried frantically to open my eyes, but it was like I was enclosed in a sealed box. I refuse to believe what she said was true. "It's not possible. You're lying. There is no way you could have done this." Voicelessly, I screamed at her.

"But I did." she was almost smug now, as if she put one over on me.

"But why? Why would you do this to me?"

"Because you were going to leave me. If not today, someday. You would eventually walk away. They always leave, so I decided to take control."

As she said those words, I felt a hand grasp around me, but that couldn't be right. My whole body seemed to rest in the palm of her hand and her fingers wrapped around me, just like when her hand held my cock. Then I felt her lips as she kissed the top of my head. Which felt like she'd just kissed the tip of my prick.

The sensation disappeared, and I instinctively knew she was licking her lips like she did every time she gave me head. Sure enough, her moistened lips engulfed my head.

I didn't want to be aroused, yet I couldn't help myself. I could feel that telltale feeling of fullness throughout my new body, as if I was getting an erection.

Her mouth eased off my head. "Well, you don't taste as good as you did in real life, but I'll get used to it. Maybe I'll get some flavoured lube?"

Amelia Dax

I felt myself go airborne, and then I was nudging at what I knew was her entrance. Don't ask me how I knew the difference between that and her mouth, but I did.

Our conversation must have made her horny, because she was soaking wet, she took me in easily.

Maneuvered by her fingers, I slid in and out of her tight channel. I felt vibrations radiate out from my core until my whole body started whirring against her skin.

She must have found the remote because I kept changing the speed of my shaking again and again until she found her favourite one.

I recognized it from when we used her other toys.

That's when it hit me. The realization that I wasn't her only toy.

She had others.

My brain suddenly overloaded with horror, wondering who else was encapsulated in her toys. What other ex-boyfriends of hers had I manhandled into her snatch every time I grabbed one of her other dildos?

"Unbidden, the memory of her pleasing herself on her bed came to my mind. In that moment, I'd stood in the doorway and watched her as she got herself off. Never once dreaming that eventually, I'd be encased in silicone with someone else thrusting me between her legs.

"Focus." She ordered, bringing me back to the present.

Obediently, I imagined her circling her breasts with her fingers and pinching her nipples until they were stiff while she pushed the toy inside right up to my fake balls on the bottom. Her pace quickened as she maneuvered me, swiveling my new body this way and that. Pulsing it in halfway to rub the ribbed edge of my glans against her g-spot until I could feel her inner muscles clench around me.

88

Amelia Dax

I heard her scream of pleasure and felt the rush of my orgasm. No idea how or why. I just felt the full body rush and her cries of joy.

The buzzing continued after my release. Long after, she pulled me out and threw me onto the bed. It took forever until she caught her breath and remembered to turn me off.

"You're not quite as good as you were in real life," she said, as if it were a compliment to my old self. "But at least you'll never leave me this way." Then I heard her humming as the connection between us faded as she walked away.

Amelia Dax

Amelia Dax

HOT HITCHHIKER

She stood on the side of the road with her thumb extended.

Normally, I wouldn't stop to pick up a hitchhiker. Hell, I can't even tell you the last time I saw a hitchhiker on the road.

It was pouring rain, and she looked like she'd been out there for a while.

Maybe she got into a fight with her boyfriend, and he kicked her out of the car. I mean, some men were assholes.

I slowed down as I passed her and then pressed on the brakes when I saw she wasn't dressed for the weather. It was late September, and she wore a light jacket, jeans, and flip-flops. She was soaked to the skin.

Although, to be fair, until the rain started this afternoon, it had been an unseasonably warm couple of days.

When my car pulled to a stop, I threw it into reverse and backed up a few feet, so she didn't have to run as far to get in.

She opened the door and peeked in. Not just at me, the driver, but she also took a quick glance in the back seat to see if anyone else was in the vehicle with me. When she saw I was alone, her shoulders sagged in relief.

Yes, I was a man, but I was less than intimidating. I was the epitome of a computer geek with fine-boned, thin shoulders, and my Irish heritage shining through with pale skin and ginger hair.

Tonight, I was grateful for my appearance because as soon as she saw how unintimidating I was she relaxed and got in my car, shutting the door quickly behind her against the weather.

"Thank you." She said with relief evident in her voice. "I thought I was going to be out there for hours."

"Not a problem. It's a miserable night." I glanced over at her. "Why are you on the side of the road? Did your car breakdown?" I was hopeful it was something I could help her with. I may not look like a mechanic, but I knew engines.

"No." she wiped at the corner of her eye as if it was more than just rain streaming down her face. "My boyfriend and I got into a fight."

"And he left you on the side of the road on a night like this?"

She flinched at the anger in my voice.

"He's got a temper. Usually, it's not so bad, but we were out, and there was a group of guys flirting with me. He insisted I was flirting back when really, I was just trying to play nice so I could get out from where they cornered me against the bar."

"He didn't come to rescue you?"

"He thought I liked it. He assumed I was inviting them."

I looked at her clothes and sure she wore a crop top and jeans, but she had a long baggy army jacket on over the top. Usually, if the girls were out clubbing, they wore skintight dresses and showed far more skin than this woman did. She looked more girl next door than huntress.

"Where do you need to go? I'll make sure you get home safe." I said as I put the car in gear and pulled away from the side of the road. I assumed I was going in the right direction since that's the way she had been headed.

"It's not too far up the road. We were pretty close when he made me get out of his car. I think that's why he didn't circle back, because he figured I could make it home on my own."

"Are you sure that's where you want to go? Is there somewhere else I can take you, so you don't have to deal with him tonight?"

She looked over at me and even in the dim light from the dashboard, I could see the red rims around her eyes. Her smile was melancholy. "I'd love that more than you know, but if I'm not home tonight, there will be even more hell to pay tomorrow."

"Okay. Let's get you where you need to be." I said as I continued driving.

We'd only gone about a click down the road when my engine stalled.

A quick look at my gas gauge surprised the hell out of me because it said the tank was empty. I'd just filled it two days ago and hadn't gone anywhere besides home and work, except for tonight when I had the urge to go for a drive after supper. There was no reason for my tank to be empty. I was thoroughly confused because the car usually dinged when I had thirty-five kilometers left in the tank. I worried something else was wrong with the engine, but the dashboard was lit up as clear as day. I coasted off the road and steered back onto the gravel sidewalk.

"It doesn't seem like I'm going to be much help after all." I said just before we were plunged into darkness sixty seconds after the engine stopped.

"Hey, I'm still better off than I was three minutes ago." She said. "At least now I have shelter and your car is warm." Despite her claim, she was shivering.

"I think I've got a blanket in the back seat. Hang on."
I asked her to hold my phone's flashlight steady as I
reached over the centre console and pushed my knapsack
aside to retrieve the blanket underneath it.

"What else is back there?" she asked curiously, eying
the big plastic bin behind her seat.

"I am a complete geek." The heat of embarrassment
crept up my face. "I keep one of my small telescopes and
its extra lenses in the car so I can go star gazing on a whim."
It's not like I ever have anyone sit in the back seat, anyway.
I tried to keep the bitterness at bay. Most of my friends were
married with children. I was the lone bachelor in my friend
group from high school.

Always the groomsman, never the groom. The familiar
joke came unbidden to my mind.

I handed her the blanket, thankful that I thought to turn
on the seat warmer as soon as she got into the vehicle. At
least she wasn't battling the cold seat to retain her body
heat.

"Aren't you cold?" she asked as I got her all bundled
up, surprised at how dry she was already.

"I'm okay." I assured her. "I wasn't the one standing
out in the rain."

"Still." She hesitated. "Why don't you lean over the
centre, and we can share the blanket? Sharing body heat
will keep us both warmer."

"Okay." I stammered, more than a little confused. This
wasn't my life. Pretty girls like her usually didn't want a
chance to get close to me. Normally, they chose one of my
friends when we went out as a group. When I was alone, I
was practically invisible to the fairer sex.

"Hang on, this isn't working." She tossed the blanket
toward me. "This centre thing is digging into my ribs. I

don't understand why they don't make bench seats anymore." She grumbled as she twisted around in her seat, got up on her knees and plunked herself down on my cup holder.

At that point, my brain started working. "Hang on a second." I reached between my legs, thankful that my car had manual seat adjustments, and pushed my seat back as far as it would go. "There." I said.

Once she saw what I had done, she put her hand on my dash and the other hand on the raised storage compartment part of my centre console and moved her ass over to sit on my lap with her back against the door. It took a few minutes to rearrange the blanket over us and ensure it was tucked in to prevent drafts. Honestly, you'd think it was February at how meticulously we completed the task.

"This is much better." she said as she rested her head on my shoulder and gave a contented sigh.

I had one arm behind her back, trying to cushion her from the armrest. I wasn't sure what to do with my other arm, so I draped it over her shins. I let my hand hang loose to avoid touching her inappropriately. Seemed silly since she didn't seem worried about it from the way she cuddled into me.

She shivered again, so I started running my hand up and down her arm closest to the steering wheel, hoping to keep her from getting a chill.

"You are such a nice guy," she said. "Most guys would have already had their tongues down my throat and their hand between my legs."

I nearly choked on thin air. "Er. Um, yeah. No, that's never been me." I stuttered.

"Why not?" she asked, as if there was a real question in her mind.

"Well, I…" I wasn't really sure what to say. Did she not get a good look at me when she got in my car? "Well, I'm not the most masculine guy… and my mom raised me to respect women. Well, to respect everybody, but women particularly, because men use their size and strength when they shouldn't." I laughed. "She saw my red hair and assumed I'd have a temper. She had no idea I would take after her in body size instead of my dad."

"I think I'd like your mom." her tone was decisive. "She did a good job raising you." She leaned in close, wrapped her outer arm around my shoulder, and gave me a kiss on the cheek.

"Plus, you said you had a boyfriend with a mean streak." I reminded her.

"Ex-boyfriend." Her expression was grim. "I do not have a boyfriend now. Not if he thought it was all right to leave me on the side of the road in the middle of the night when it's raining. I'll go home tonight, but I'm going to leave him tomorrow. I've had enough."

"Good." I said. "I'm glad to hear that. No one deserves to be treated that way." I was trying really hard not to notice that she hadn't moved back, and she was still pressed up tight against me. I hoped like hell she couldn't feel the steel rod growing between my legs.

But the way she was smirking, I think she knew what exactly she was doing to me. Then she wiggled her ass, erasing all doubt.

"You have a stiffy and you're still not making a move." Her voice was incredulous.

"Keeping you warm and dry and safe is more important than getting my rocks off." Shit, even I heard how prim and proper that sounded.

Amelia Dax

Then she laughed. The sound filled my car as she struggled to catch her breath, which honestly made me giggle too, and the two of us fed off of each other's laughter until tears streamed down our cheeks.

"Oh my God, I think I've fallen completely irrevocably in love with you." she hugged me again. Closer this time and when she pulled back, she kissed me full on the lips.

It was so unexpected that I was still mid laugh, and our teeth crashed together. I'm sure I felt the tang of blood on my tongue as she started kissing me gently.

"Sorry." She said between featherlight kisses. "That was my fault. Let me kiss it and make it better."

She tasted like beer and bubble gum. A surprisingly intoxicating combination as we explored each other's mouths.

I wasn't a virgin, but I also hadn't had much practice. I was grateful she was an excellent kisser as she nipped and teased at my lips and allowed my tongue to slip past and deepen the contact.

Just as I slid my hand around her front, I froze.

My mom's voice echoed through my brain. "Don't take advantage."

My passenger must have sensed my sudden hesitation because she reached for my wrist and brought my hand under the hem of her crop top to cover her breast. She wasn't wearing a bra. Then she arched her back to give me more room to move my hands.

I pushed her top up over her breasts and bent my head to kiss her nipple. It was an awkward angle until I remembered to flip down the back of my seat to give us more room.

"Slide back." She ordered while lifting herself off my lap and then twisted around in the tight confines to kneel in the passenger seat.

My seat was almost flat and as I did as she asked, I realized I had somehow lost my pants from around my hips. The waist bound my thighs together. The teeth of the zipper dug into my legs just above my knee, but honestly, I couldn't care less. My cock was in her hand, and she bent over to lick up the long drool of pre-cum sliding down its length.

She kissed the tip and looked at me with a very satisfied grin before lowering her mouth again and engulfing my entire head.

This wasn't the first blow job I'd ever received, but dear God, it was the best. For once, I didn't mind that I wasn't as well-endowed as some of the other guys, because she was able to take me entirely into her mouth. I could feel her lips brushing against my balls as she swallowed me whole.

I couldn't help it. My hips bucked up, shoving me further in her mouth.

She gagged for a split second before she swallowed and kept her lips wrapped around me.

I was so sensitive, I felt every flex of her tongue. "I'm gonna come." I warned her, embarrassingly fast.

Her only response was to slide her fingers around the base of my balls, to set me off.

My hips thrust in a jerky motion beyond my control as I spewed my load down her throat. When I was done, I was panting heavily to get my breath back. By the time I finally opened my eyes, I was amazed to see she'd somehow already removed her pants and had climbed over the console, lowering her knees on either side of me.

She hovered above my still rock-hard cock.

I panicked. "You don't have to. That's not why I picked you up." I told her.

"I know." she smiled. "He's already accused me of cheating on him. I might as well do the deed, and you are such a lovely man. I feel safe with you." She lowered herself until just my tip slipped past her outer lips. "I want to be with you. Need to be with you even if it's just for right now." and with that, she slid down over my prick.

I fought the urge to come again. It's been over a year since I've had sex with anything besides my hand and she was so much better. I reached up to hold her steady.

The lower edge of my palms rested on her rib cage so that she could lean against me while my thumbs traced the outline of her nipples as she slid herself back and forth over my cock.

Up and down. Side to side. She moved in sexy little rotations. When she pressed herself close to my pubic bone, and got the pressure just right, she moaned, "Oh God, that feels good. Then she leaned forward enough and thrust her tits in my face.

I obeyed her unspoken command and latched on to her with my mouth and suckled while pressing her breasts together so I could reach them both.

This time, I held on. I found my feet again and thrust up inside her as she moved over me, moaning as if I was the best thing she'd ever felt.

Her breath came in quick gasps. She was close. I moved my hand between us. A move I'd read about in a romance book after my last breakup, trying to understand what women were looking for. I placed my thumb at the top of her slit and found that little hard nub that they always talked about. I pressed down just a little, and she shot up. Almost cracked her head on the car's roof.

"Oh my God, keep doing that." Her breath grew even more frantic.

I felt her inner muscles clench around my cock.

"Oh, my God. Don't stop." She rose up and grabbed onto the holy shit bar above the driver's door and braced her other hand on the back of the passenger seat.

I watched in fascination at the surprise on her face when she came. The way her inner muscles gripped my cock and the extra moisture flooding from her set me off, too.

I let loose with a howl as she collapsed against me. We were still in complete darkness aside from a streetlight a hundred or so meters away.

I slumped back against my lowered seat, cradling her protectively against me, our chests still heaving from the exertion.

"Can I keep you?" she whispered. "Are you even real or are you an apparition, someone to save me from the hell my life has become?"

I chuckled. "I'm nothing special, just a Good Samaritan who saw a damsel in distress on the side of the road and gave her some place warm and dry."

She shifted herself over me with a giggle, and my softened dick slid out from her with a plop. "Dry is not the word I'd use." Her voice grew serious. "You are my knight in shining armor."

At that moment, a set of headlights came up the hill behind us.

"Thank you," she said as she climbed back over to the passenger seat.

I raised the lever to bring my seat upright.

Then, several things happened at once. The vehicle behind us pulled off to the side and slowed to a stop. My car's engine started, and she disappeared.

The door hadn't opened, but she was gone.

A quick look at my gas gauge showed that I still had half a tank of gas, as red and blue lights pierced the darkness.

A dark figure with a flashlight approached, and I noticed it had stopped raining.

Frantically, I leaned forward to hide my cock. My pants were still around my thighs, and my interior smelled of sex. It hadn't been a dream.

I lowered my window when the person knocked on the glass, still unsure how to explain my situation and not get arrested for public indecency. To my surprise, he was laughing.

"I see you met Daisy." His casual comment stunned me.

Was that her name? Ashamed, I realized I hadn't even asked. Wait a minute. She disappeared before he approached my car. How did he even know?

"I'll give you a minute to get your pants up." Still chuckling, he turned his back.

I wasted no time getting dressed. "What did you mean about meeting Daisy?"

"Gorgeous blonde, crop top, bellbottom jeans and a faded army jacket, abandoned on the side of the road by her abusive boyfriend?"

"Yes," I answered. Suddenly, I wasn't sure I wanted to know how he knew all of this.

"I don't know how to tell you this he said, but you got ghosted."

"Well, she left without saying goodbye, but…" my voice trailed off.

"No, I mean she's a ghost." He wasn't laughing anymore. "In 1973, Daisy McHenry was out with her boyfriend, when they got into a fight. He was drunk and angry. He just reached over, opened the door, and pushed her out without slowing down. That was back before wearing seatbelts was law. She died on impact."

I nodded. "She told me they got in a fight because men cornered her at the bar, and he accused her of flirting."

"Yeah, that's what the original report says."

"But… she was hitchhiking tonight. I saw her. She was there." Panic tinged my voice. Was I losing my mind?

"Yes, you absolutely saw her. That's why we've started doing patrols in this area because on nights like this, she usually makes at least one appearance. More than one guy has gotten himself lost in the woods because he went looking for her."

"She was a ghost?"

He nodded. "I'm afraid so." He paused. "I can give you a silver lining of sorts. She only appears to nice, stand-up types of guys, so consider this your thumbs up from the spirit world."

AFTERWORD

If you enjoyed this story, please leave a review on Goodreads or your favourite book retailer. Your reviews help more than you can imagine.

Stay Sexy,
Amelia

Amelia Dax

OTHER BOOKS BY AMELIA DAX

Find them at your favourite retailer
https://linktr.ee/ameliadax

Earth Outpost 6-9

Nestled near the asteroid belt between Mars and Jupiter, Earth has 360 monitoring stations. Damian and Elin are stationed at Outpost 6-9. A coincidence? Perhaps not. They will do anything to make their interstellar guests feel welcome... ANYTHING.

Eventually, they learn their role isn't just fun and games. The universe is vast, humans are weak, and soon they'll need all the interstellar friends they can get.

Horni-Culture

What if that little house on the prairie had plants you could use as sex toys?

The world as we know it has ended. Those who are left, struggle to survive. Until they discover a mysterious species of plants that help them find a little joy and a lot of orgasms.

Amelia Dax

Merry Elfin Christmas

Two Christmas stories your mom definitely never read to you at bedtime. In Shelf-less Shenanigans, Herald, an Observer Elf, delivers an extra helping of Christmas Cheer to a divorced woman spending her first Christmas alone. Then we head to the North Pole for Reclaiming Mrs. Claus, where a few enthusiastic elves get Mrs. Claus all fired up to reclaim her family's legacy from a wayward Santa.

If you enjoy fun, sexy times, you'll love these short story series.

Get my complete book list at:

Amelia Dax
Author Bio

Forgettable by day and incredible at night, Amelia Dax takes inspiration from the world around us and beyond. She crafts fun stories of lust and satisfaction.

@ameliadaxerotica

amelia@ameliadax.com

www.ingramcontent.com/pod-product-compliance
Lightning Source LLC
Chambersburg PA
CBHW020744130626
46554CB00006B/2145